A DANGEROUS FAN

He was almost through his pile of envelopes when he came across a fan letter that had been mailed from Sesa to his publisher in New York. He could tell by the Sesa postmark—there was no return address. He was surprised. Sesa was a small town of only ten thousand. It was true he got letters from all over America—the whole world for that matter—but even with the volume of mail he received, the odds of his getting a letter from his hometown were slim. He fingered the letter thoughtfully before opening it.

"What's the matter?" Ann asked, looking up.

"Someone from Sesa sent this."

"What does it say?"

"I don't know."

Ann was intrigued. "Open it. Read it."

Marvin tore open the envelope. The note was only one sentence long, typed on clean white paper in capital letters.

I KNOW WHO YOU ARE.

"I know who you are," Marvin whispered aloud, and he felt his heart skip a beat.

Books by Christopher Pike

BURY ME DEEP
CHAIN LETTER 2: THE ANCIENT EVIL
DIE SOFTLY
FALL INTO DARKNESS
FINAL FRIENDS #1: THE PARTY
FINAL FRIENDS #2: THE DANCE
FINAL FRIENDS #3: THE GRADUATION
GIMME A KISS
LAST ACT
MASTER OF MURDER
REMEMBER ME
SCAVENGER HUNT
SEE YOU LATER
SPELLBOUND
WHISPER OF DEATH
WITCH

Available from ARCHWAY Paperbacks

Christopher Pike

Master of Murder

AN ARCHWAY PAPERBACK
Published by POCKET BOOKS

New York   London   Toronto   Sydney   Tokyo   Singapore

AN ARCHWAY PAPERBACK *Original*

An Archway Paperback published by
POCKET BOOKS, a division of Simon & Schuster Inc.
1230 Avenue of the Americas, New York, NY 10020

ISBN: 0-671-69059-0

First Archway Paperback printing July 1992

10 9 8 7 6 5 4 3 2 1

AN ARCHWAY PAPERBACK and colophon are registered trademarks of Simon & Schuster Inc.

Cover art by Brian Kotzky

Printed in the U.S.A.

IL 8+

For Brian

Master of Murder

CHAPTER 1

Marvin Summer sat in his English class watching the beautiful and wonderful Shelly Quade. She was two seats up on his left, and she was reading a Mack Slate young adult thriller. She was, in fact, finishing the latest book in Mr. Slate's hysterically popular *The Mystery of Silver Lake* series. From the expression on Shelly's face it looked as if she was really into the book. Up front a student was reading her short story to the class. Not far away their teacher, Mrs. Jackson, was taking notes on a yellow pad and passing judgment on the student's story. But Marvin could see that Shelly was in another world. The world of Slate's mysteries, where brave and beautiful young girls—like Shelly herself, Marvin thought—single-handedly battled the forces of darkness.

Marvin knew that world well. He *was* Mack Slate, he really was. He was one of the most popular writers in the country. His books sold millions of copies. He was only seventeen, still in high school, but already rich. Three of his books were currently being produced into movies. His series was the talk in malls and schools everywhere. Who killed Silver Lake's heroine, Ann McGaffer? There were many suspects. Had it been Ann's violent father—Bill McGaffer? Or Ann's jealous boyfriend—Clyde Fountain? Or possibly Ann's disturbed younger brother—Harold McGaffer? No one knew.

Not even Marvin Summer.

The final installment of his series was due *now*. His editor's calls were getting more desperate daily. If he didn't send in the manuscript soon the book couldn't possibly be ready for a February release. Then the publishing house's whole advertising campaign would be screwed up. But Marvin hadn't even started on the book. He had no idea how the story was going to end.

The pressure on him was intense.

But that was only one of his problems. He had others, oh yes. His life was just as complicated as the life of one of his fictional characters. He was thankful that, at least, he hadn't killed anybody, and that no one was trying to kill him. But like the heroine in his series, he did have a violent father who didn't mind roughing him up some. He no longer lived at home now. And also like most of his characters, Marvin was in romantic turmoil.

The source of that turmoil was the one and only

Shelly Quade. They had gone out briefly a year ago—five times to be exact. She had seemed to like him a lot, but she'd also been seeing a guy named Harry Paster at the time. Off and on, Marvin had thought, but maybe more on than he realized. When Harry had committed suicide the previous November by diving off a cliff at the local lake, she had fallen into a deep depression and withdrew. Poor old Harry—never was one to laugh much. Marvin was not a pushy person, so he left Shelly alone, figuring she'd see him when she wanted. But it was now a new November and she continued to avoid him. He wrote about unfulfilled teen love all the time, and he wished he weren't writing from direct experience. Just looking at her made him sad.

Shelly had hair and she had skin—both lovely. He could close his eyes and remember what it felt like to run his fingers through her long brown silky strands. The last time they had gone out, the only time they had kissed, he had held her hair and touched her skin. Being a writer he knew how overworked it was to say a girl's face glowed, but Shelly's really did, along with her neck, arms, and other parts. Her smile also shone—she was a regular Christmas tree. He had never written about her, though, because he wrote to escape, and if he spent all night dwelling on her he would have ended up in the same boat as poor Harry. Except Harry had not ended up in a boat. He had hit cold black water when he died in the lake.

Ah, Marvin observed with satisfaction, Shelly was biting her lower lip. She must be at a tense part.

Actually the whole end of the book had been tense. Even writing the damn thing had made him a nervous wreck. He had felt nervous kissing her, too, but that had been a good kind of anxiety. Of course when he'd kissed her good night a year ago he never realized it would be for the last time.

And maybe it hadn't been. Maybe he would kiss her again.

He intended to ask her out again.

Today, in fact, if he didn't have a heart attack first.

"Marvin?" Mrs. Jackson called, and it didn't sound as if it was for the first time. He must have spaced out. "Are you ready to read your story?"

Yes, but are you ready to listen, you old fart?

"Yes, ma'am," he said, reaching for the computer-printed pages on top of his desk. Shelly had glanced back at him when Mrs. Jackson called his name. She smiled slightly at him and slowly closed her book. She was so cute—it made him sick. He smiled back and climbed unsteadily to his feet. He had spent all of thirty minutes that morning completing his English assignment. He had learned long ago that it didn't matter how long he spent writing something for Mrs. Jackson—he'd get a lousy grade anyway. It was the topics she chose—they were absurd. He didn't understand why she didn't let them write what they wanted. Today's topic was "What it feels like to be an animal and discover yourself." Mrs. Jackson was hopeful that they could work in a moral. Marvin never worried about morals in his books. His characters were happy if they lived until the last page.

"What's the name of your story?" Mrs. Jackson asked as Marvin made his way to the front of the room.

"It's called 'The Becoming of Seymour the Frog,'" he said.

Mrs. Jackson blinked in surprise. "Is a frog an animal, Marvin? I think it's an amphibian."

"I don't know much about frogs."

"Then why did you write about one?" she asked.

He spoke sincerely. "I was hoping to learn about them as I wrote."

Someone in the room snickered. Marvin thought it might have been Shelly. Mrs. Jackson, however, took the remark at face value and nodded approval.

"We should learn something new with each assignment," she said. She wrote down his title on her pad. "You may begin."

Marvin glanced down at his paper and cleared his throat. He realized that not a single person in the class had the slightest interest in what he was about to read, and that ten seconds after he was done they would have forgotten every word he said. Therefore, he didn't read with much enthusiasm.

"Seymour the Frog lived in a dirty pond outside an abandoned steel mill in Pittsburgh, Pennsylvania. He was not a bad-looking frog by frog standards, but there wasn't a chance in hell that a princess was going to stop and kiss him. He was green and covered with warts and he couldn't eat a fly without getting a bad case of the hiccups. His was the life of frogs everywhere. He swam in his pond, sat in the mud in the sun, and prayed a cat didn't eat him.

"Yet Seymour had a dream. He dreamed that one day he would fly. Hardly an afternoon went by that a flock of birds didn't fly overhead. Seymour would stare up at them with such longing that he thought he would burst. Ah, to be free of the earth, he thought. To be able to go where he wished without fear of hungry cats.

"He tried flapping his slimy frog legs, but quickly discovered they didn't work the way wings did. He tried other tricks to get into the air. He climbed the highest rocks he could find around the pond, and threw himself off them with great bravado. But all he ended up doing was bruising his belly when he flopped into the water. He just could not stay airborne.

"Then one day he saw a most remarkable sight. A child's yellow balloon floated over his pond. At first it stayed close to the ground, but then an updraft caught it and it was swept as high as any bird Seymour had ever seen. Seymour took special note of the balloon. It was round and filled only with air. Yet it had no wings and still could fly! He got excited. What if he filled himself with air? Wouldn't he also be able to fly? At last, he thought, he had found the key to his escape.

"Seymour began to suck in huge drafts of air, taking in more and more without releasing the others. He sucked and he sucked and soon his belly began to bloat out. Then his chest and his face expanded, and finally even his legs began to swell.

He bobbled off the ground. He was so excited that he opened his mouth a tiny bit and accidentally let some air escape. But he managed to contain himself and breathed even deeper and harder and was rewarded when he finally lifted off the ground. In minutes he was floating a dozen feet above his pond. Then a gentle breeze came along and took him even higher. Seymour was ecstatic. He was flying! He was a flying frog! Probably the first one in the history of the human race. Oh, happy day. He could fly anywhere he wished.

"Right then Seymour noticed a flock of birds flying overhead. He was eager to join them but they were even higher than he was. So he forced in more air, and even though the pressure was beginning to hurt his chest, he didn't stop until he was floating at the same height as the birds. They were only a hundred feet away and coming right toward him. He was so excited to be in their company. He wanted to impress them with what a great flyer he was. So he drew in one final huge breath. But his green wart-covered skin had stretched as far as it could stretch, and this deep breath was the last breath of Seymour's life.

"Seymour popped. He exploded like a green balloon set on top of a lit candle. His head went one way and his legs another, and there was blood everywhere. It was a real mess. Seeing him explode the birds got all excited. They were hungry, and as Seymour's guts fell to the rocks beside his pond, the birds swept down and ate what was left of him. Then they flew away, taking pieces of Seymour with them. So, in a way, Seymour got what he had wished for most—to be a bird."

Marvin stopped reading and looked up. A few of the people in class had listened after all. They were grinning. He could see Shelly sitting toward the back, laughing softly. Although his classmates' reactions were nothing compared to the adoration his books brought him, he was filled with pleasure.

Then he glanced over at Mrs. Jackson. She was scowling.

"Are you quite through, Mr. Summer?" she asked.

"Yeah. Did you like it?"

She consulted her notes, her breathing rapid. "In your story you mention that the balloon Seymour spotted was filled with air. It's my understanding that balloons that float are filled with helium. Is that not correct?"

"The story is kind of told from the point of view of a frog," Marvin said patiently. "I doubt a frog would know anything about helium."

Mrs. Jackson continued to study her notes. "You also use the line that Seymour was the first flying frog in the history of the human race. If you are telling the story from the point of view of a frog, why do you talk about the history of the human race?"

"I threw that line in for humor."

Mrs. Jackson looked up. "Pardon?"

"It was a joke, ma'am. The whole story is supposed to be funny."

"I suppose you think the disgusting ending, when the birds eat Seymour's *guts,* is funny?"

"Yeah." Marvin turned to the rest of the class. "Didn't you guys think so?"

Murmurs of approval went around. Shelly continued to laugh softly. Mrs. Jackson stuck out her hand for his paper.

"We don't grade democratically in this class," she said.

"I think we should," Marvin muttered, handing over his story.

"Pardon?"

"Nothing."

"I heard you anyway." Mrs. Jackson reached for her red pen, which she saved for the fateful marking of grades. He didn't much care what she wrote. Given his previous scores, he was going to just pass the class. Yet she surprised him by writing a huge B at the top of his paper. She handed it back to him with a wink, a gesture he would have thought her incapable of. "The story did have a certain flair," she admitted. "I felt sorry for Seymour at the end. If you learn to control yourself, Marvin, you might make a writer someday."

"Thank you," he said, accepting his paper. But he didn't take her advice to heart. He was already a bigger writer than anybody in the state. Besides, it was when he was out of control that he wrote his best—when the *power* flowed. But he couldn't have explained that power to Mrs. Jackson any more than he could have explained his love for Shelly to himself. Creativity and love—they were two sides of the same coin, two rivers that flowed in the same direction.

Into the same lake.

He didn't know why he was thinking of Harry now. Probably because he was going to ask Shelly out, and the memory of Harry was the main reason she might say no. Yet if the stories were true Shelly had already started to date again—a football stud at school named Triad Tyler. Triad—he sounded like a structure, a building of some kind. Marvin had noticed her talking to him a few times but had never actually seen them exchanging physical affections. Marvin had even spoken to Triad a couple of times himself, although not about Shelly. Triad wanted to buy his motorcycle, which Marvin prized almost as much as his word processor. He had told Triad no, but the guy kept asking.

Marvin took his story and walked back to his seat. As he passed Shelly she picked up her Mack Slate thriller. She didn't glance up as he passed, but did mutter under her breath.

"Nice," she said. "Gross."

"Glad you liked it," he replied. Her two words gave an incredible boost to his confidence. He really must ask her out. He vowed to do it as soon as the bell rang. He was always making vows like that to himself.

His wasn't the last reading of the day. Two more people followed him. The first had a story about a dog and the second, a cat; they were really imaginative with their choice of animals. Marvin went back to staring at Shelly Quade and heard not a word they said.

When the class finally ended, Marvin gathered together his books and maneuvered himself behind

Shelly as she walked down the hallway. He wanted to come casually up at her side, start a casual conversation, and then sweep her into the janitors' closet and make passionate love to her. No, he had better skip that last part. He had to be—well, casual. He had to be cool.

"Hi," he said as he caught up with her.

She looked over. Such lovely eyes. Green around the rims, brown in the centers. Big enough to take all of him in at a glance. She batted her eyelashes and he was practically blown away. God, what a sap he'd become sitting in class and staring at her the last three months. The worst thing—or maybe it was the best thing—was that they shared the next class as well.

"Hello, Marvin," she said.

She had said his name! She remembered who he was! He was off to an excellent start, he thought. Of course, it would have been weird if she'd forgotten who he was after they had gone out five times. He had to remind himself that just because she was young and pretty did not necessarily mean that she suffered from amnesia.

"What's happening?" he asked.

"The usual," she said. "What's happening with you?"

Well, my latest novel was just on The New York Times *best-seller list—the first young adult book in the history of publishing to make it. I recently received a royalty check in the mail, in the high six figures. Girls everywhere—and you're one of them —are reading my books and getting tremors of fear and ecstasy deep in their insides. Oh, yeah, and I'm madly in love with you. Other than that, life is pretty mundane.*

"Nothing," he replied. He took a breath. He should just ask the question now and be done with it. A bunch of small talk wasn't going to change her opinion of him—she already knew him. She would either say yes or no—it was as simple as that. But asking her, forming the words and flinging them into the space between them—there was nothing simple about that. "Shelly," he muttered.

"Yes?"

Damn! I said her name too seriously. I sound desperate. I am desperate. I have to be cool.

He nodded to his book in her hand. "What are you reading?"

"Slate's series." She glanced at the book. The artist who did his covers was one of the best in New York. But it was Marvin who decided what should be on them. He was always late with his manuscripts, and his publisher needed the covers far in advance of the actual publication dates, so he had to figure out what would look good on the cover before he had even written a word of the book. "Do you read his stuff?" she asked.

"I'm familiar with it."

Shelly shook her head. "He's a genius. Once I pick up his books, I can't put them down."

Marvin felt warm with pleasure even though he got tons of letters each week that said exactly what Shelly had just said. "He does have an incredible imagination," he remarked.

"Are you reading this series?" Shelly asked.

"Yeah."

"Did you read the last one?"

"Yeah." He added, "I wonder how it'll end."

She was suddenly excited. "I bet it's going to be great."

This last comment didn't fill him with quite the same pleasure. Expectations across the country were so high—he was bound to disappoint a lot of people.

"We'll see," he said. They were almost at their next class. He felt about as nervous as an individual could. He had sweat coming out of pores on his body—pores he hadn't even had early that morning. He knew what his problem was. He had put Shelly on a pedestal. He kept telling himself she was just a girl—but that wasn't true. She wasn't a girl—she was *the* girl. She could have been *his* girl. He tried desperately to think of a witty line to open the "date line" of conversation, but none came. He should have prepared a few ahead of time. "Shelly?" he said.

"Yes?"

He cleared his throat. "I want to be a writer someday."

She gave him a knowing look. "I remember."

He was surprised. "What do you remember?"

She spoke seriously. "The stories you used to tell me when we went out. They were wonderful. You should write them down."

He supposed he had told her a few stories. He had probably made them up at the moment, and then forgotten them. His head was full of weird tales. He was pleased she had brought up the fact that they used to date. Perhaps she was dropping a hint that she wouldn't mind dating again.

"Were any of them about frogs?" he asked.

She laughed. "That was gross. I loved it. What grade did Stonewall Jackson give you?"

"The best grade she's ever given me—a B."

"I thought she was going to give you an F." Shelly was watching him as she spoke. She had a penetrating gaze. He would have given all his next advance to know what she was thinking right then. "You wouldn't have cared, would you?" she asked.

"No," he said honestly. He was already a millionaire. It wasn't as if he had to worry about getting into a good college after he graduated.

Shelly smiled. "You're unique. Did I ever tell you that?"

He felt another surge of confidence. He would ask her out now. She would say yes. He could feel the *power,* the same power he sometimes felt when he was doing his best writing. At those times it was as if nothing could go wrong.

But something did go wrong just then. Triad Tyler suddenly stepped between them. Triad was big, strong, and handsome. He was also stupid—a wonderful combination. Marvin's most penetrating observations in life had convinced him that girls favored that combination above all others, even intelligent girls like Shelly Quade. Marvin watched with sheer disgust as Triad bumped him aside and reached out a gorilla arm to give her a squeeze.

"My baby doll," Triad said to Shelly. "How you doing?"

Shelly seemed annoyed. "I am always the same. I don't change. How are you?"

Triad took back his arm and grinned at her remark, perhaps seeing more in it than there was, probably not understanding it at all. "I'm cool. Everything's cool." He glanced over at Marvin. "Hey, when are you going to sell me that bike of yours?"

"Have you thought of going to a motorcycle dealer and buying a brand-new one?" Marvin asked. "Or even a used one? I don't own the only bike in the state of Oregon."

Triad's grin widened. "But they wouldn't give me a good deal."

"I'd charge you twice what I paid for it," Marvin assured him.

Triad slapped him on the back. "That's what I like about you, Marvin—you don't BS around. But seriously, I want that bike. I'll make you a good offer on it."

"You should sell him your bike," Shelly said.

"Why?" Marvin asked.

"Because motorcycles are dangerous," she said seriously. "That bike could get you killed."

Triad laughed. "So you don't mind if I get killed, is that it?"

Shelly smiled slyly. She reached out and patted Triad on the top of his head. "You have a lot harder skull than Marvin. I bet even your brains would bounce off the pavement."

15

"If they haven't done so already," Marvin muttered.

"I heard that," Triad told him, but he didn't appear to be put out. He turned back to Shelly. "Am I going to see you at lunch?"

Shelly spoke coolly. "I will be invisible. No one will see me."

"You're going out for lunch?" Triad asked.

"Maybe," she replied, suddenly turning left into a locker room. "'Bye, boys!"

"'Bye," they said together, surprised, watching her disappear. Triad glanced over at Marvin. "I don't understand her," he complained. "She's always darting away like that."

"Maybe she wants to get away from you," Marvin suggested. He debated asking Triad outright about the extent of their relationship, but decided he didn't want to know. He still intended to ask Shelly out, probably after the next period.

Triad stopped in midstride at Marvin's remark —his shoulders slumped forward. Marvin wondered if he had hurt Triad's feelings. For a moment the guy looked positively depressed. But then Triad shrugged and turned away. "I don't care either way," he said.

"Yeah, I know the feeling," Marvin said softly, watching him go.

That next period was speech. The teacher was Mr. Ramar, who was laid back. He had yet to make them give a single speech. What they usually did was read a book or a newspaper, or see a movie, and then talk about it together. They also wrote in a journal about whatever was on their minds. Mr.

Ramar was more into establishing good communication skills than orator skills. It was a great period to goof off in. Occasionally Marvin worked on his books in the class, but, of course, that was work he never handed in.

Shelly arrived a few seconds after the bell rang. The class chairs were arranged in a circle, and Shelly sat ninety degrees off to Marvin's right. Mr. Ramar moved around during the period. There were extra chairs, and he went from one to another, getting everyone involved in whatever they were discussing. Sometimes he sat in the corner and practiced his guitar. He was well liked by the student body and usually let the students bring up whatever they wanted to talk about.

That day several students wanted to discuss the mysterious Mack Slate and the Silver Lake series. Marvin groaned inside. This was too much.

"I started the series," Mr. Ramar said, his acoustic guitar resting on his lap. He was a short, handsome Hispanic man, about twenty-eight, in excellent physical shape. He continued, "I like it so far but I'm only up to the fourth book. I hear the fifth one's already out."

"I have it," Shelly said, holding up her copy.

"The sixth one's to be the last?" Mr. Ramar asked.

"Yeah," several students responded together, and from their expressions it was clear they could hardly wait.

"How many are reading it?" Mr. Ramar asked.

With the exception of Marvin and their current exchange student—Olga from Germany—

everyone raised a hand. Since Olga could hardly speak English—never mind read it—and Marvin had actually written the books, it was one hundred percent participation. Marvin was surprised. Even he hadn't realized how popular he was.

"I'm impressed," Mr. Ramar went on. "What is it about the books that keeps you reading them?"

At once several people gushed that they wanted to know who killed Ann McGaffer. Of course! That was the core of the series. Who had killed the beautiful and dear Ann. *Why* had she been killed? Marvin knew what a sucker people were for a mystery. He listened while the various suspects were debated. He was hoping to learn something.

First the basic facts were reviewed. Ann McGaffer was an eighteen-year-old high school senior, without question the most popular girl on the Silver Lake campus. She had it all: a handsome jock boyfriend, a rich dad, great clothes. But it was all an illusion. The kids at school resented her popularity, her boyfriend was screwing her best friend, her dad was an alcoholic and often beat her, and she had to diet constantly to fit into her far-out clothes. Then, at the end of book one, she had to go and die. Her body was found floating facedown in Silver Lake, *naked*—they loved that part, wow—tied up with barbed wire and showing signs of sexual abuse. But the police were not releasing all the details. For example, it wasn't known whether Ann had been raped. Nor was it known exactly when she had died, although she had clearly floated in the lake for at least one night. Her lovely pale skin was very cold.

Marvin started to get bored as they listed the three main suspects: Ann's sleazy boyfriend, Clyde Fountain; her hot-tempered dad, Bill McGaffer; her disturbed younger brother, Harold McGaffer. Oh, and there was Mike Madison; they shouldn't forget Mike. Ann had been sleeping with him as well as Clyde before she had bit the big one. Clyde hadn't known about that little affair, or so people thought. But Mike wasn't really a suspect, because he loved Ann and he was—well, so nice. But then maybe, the class said, it had been Mike because he was *too* nice. Yeah, add him to the list. Four major suspects, but dozens of others as well, each with their own hidden motives. The way Mack Slate had set it up, the possibilities were endless.

Marvin started to get a headache. Endless—he had gone over the plot endlessly. They were right. It could have been anybody. But then, why didn't he just make it anyone and start writing the last book? Who would know except him? But that wasn't the way he worked. He honestly believed that he didn't make up his plots, but that he *uncovered* them. It was as if they were there already somewhere in the astral ether, and God had given him a gift that allowed him to tune into them. When he worked on the plot for a story he simply put his attention on it periodically and let it unfold, and when it was right he knew it. He didn't manufacture his plots, not his best ones. Never before had a story failed to unfold, until now. But he knew in his heart that it could only have been one person who had killed Ann McGaffer. And he knew there was a reason why it could only be that one person.

But who?

"Who do you think it was, Marvin?" Mr. Ramar asked, bringing Marvin back to reality. Marvin sat up with a start.

"I don't know," he said sadly.

Mr. Ramar smiled. "Don't you want to venture a guess?"

Marvin shrugged. "Maybe Ann McGaffer committed suicide."

The class booed his idea, and for good reason. The evidence spoke for itself. Ann had been attacked. She had been tied up. How could she have tied herself up? What a ridiculous idea, they said. Marvin quickly withdrew his suggestion. He got no respect and here he was the author.

The discussion changed direction. The girls started to talk about who Mack Slate was, what he must be like. Marvin began to enjoy himself. They thought he was awesome.

"I bet he's thirty years old, dark, and handsome," an attractive redheaded girl named Sandy said, playing with her hair, a faraway look in her eyes. "I can see him in my mind. He lives in a house overlooking the ocean and goes for a walk with his dog every morning. He writes in a small cluttered room and smokes a pipe. He's not married."

"How do you know he's not married?" Mr. Ramar asked.

Sandy sighed. "I can tell by the way he writes that he's been hurt deeply in the past by one woman. She was very beautiful, but he had to leave her."

"Why did he have to leave her?" Mr. Ramar asked, amused.

"Because he knew if he stayed with her he would kill her," Sandy said as if it were obvious. "She was bad for him and he was bad for her."

"I don't think he'd kill her," Marvin said. "He's a writer, not a psychopath."

"He's a genius," Sandy snapped as if an ordinary writer and a genius had nothing in common. "All geniuses are nuts."

"I don't think he's nuts," a blond girl named Debra interrupted. "I bet he's tall and blond and has a cute blond wife and two adorable blond children—one boy and one girl. He's probably close to forty, but looks younger because he runs on the beach every morning." She smiled to herself. "I just know he's absolutely gorgeous."

Well, thank you, my dear. I happen to be free after class if you want to start on those adorable babies.

Marvin was not gorgeous and he knew it. But he believed he was handsome. Had he written about himself, he would have said he had dark features, a good-natured expression, and bewitching brown eyes. But he never did write about himself, not specifically. That was the mistake they made—they thought they knew him by what he wrote. It was true parts of him were in every one of his stories, but those parts were plugged into so many different characters they couldn't be restructured into one whole person. In other words, he wasn't in the book, he *was* the book, all parts of it, even the badly written parts, which just went to show he was as lazy as the next guy.

"Why do you both think he lives next to the beach?" Mr. Ramar asked.

"Because he gets his inspiration from the ocean," Sandy said.

"Because he's rich and can afford it," Debra said.

"But is the ocean in many of his books?" Mr. Ramar asked. "His series takes place in a town much like our town. Maybe he lives near a lake."

Marvin chuckled to himself and glanced out the window. Two points for Mr. Ramar. Marvin could see Lake Sesa from where he was sitting, a mile away through the trees and meadows that surrounded Sesa High. It was smaller than Silver Lake, but only a little.

"If Mack Slate lives on a lake," Ms. Sandy Serious said with an air of indignation, "it's bottomless."

"I think Mack Slate's not his real name," Shelly said. "It sounds like a pen name to me."

"Why's that?" Mr. Ramar asked.

Shelly shrugged. "It just does." Then she giggled. "His real name's probably something like Irving Dumlop or Fred Smith. Something boring like that. In fact he's probably an old fart who can't get laid."

Marvin burst out laughing, along with the rest of the class. Shelly's remark only intensified debate over Mack Slate's personal life. It went on until the bell rang. By then Mack Slate was a transvestite living in the Sahara Desert with a herd of camels for pets and an illegitimate son who was actually a clone of one of his murder victims.

Once again Marvin caught up with Shelly after she left class. His nerves were still taut. Her remark about being unable to get laid had made him laugh, but the truth of it hurt as well. The sex scenes he wrote had been read by millions of kids but he had never done it himself.

Which just goes to show you can't believe everything you read.

"Shelly?" he said, coming up beside her.

Those eyes again. Looking at him with amusement. "Are you following me, sir?" she asked.

"No, I'm stalking you."

Her arm brushed against his. Could have been an accident. Could have been a divine omen. "Like a Mack Slate villain?" she asked.

He forced a chuckle. "You really think he's an old fart?"

"I think he's probably different than we imagine." She paused. "Did you want to ask me something?"

"Yeah, I did." He had to stop there. He was having trouble with his tongue.

She waited. "What?"

He bit his tongue. Ouch—but there, now it was awake. He opened his mouth, coughed. "Do you want to go out?" he asked finally.

"When?"

"I don't know. Tonight?"

"Sure."

"Great." He took a deep breath. She had said sure. That was the same as yes. She had said yes! God, this was great. This was wonderful. This moment he would have to write about someday. "What would you like to do?" he asked.

She gave him a dear Shelly Quade look, which was very dear indeed. "I would like to have a great time. You decide what we should do."

"I'll give it serious thought." He knew he would think about nothing else the rest of the day. "What time should I pick you up?"

"Six. Is six good?"

"Yeah."

She made a face. "Are we going on your bike?"

"We don't have to." Not that he had another mode of transportation immediately available, although he supposed he could take his mother's car. If she didn't know about it.

"I don't mind," she said quickly.

"I'll get a car."

"Maybe we can go in my mother's car," she offered.

"We'll work it out. It'll be all right."

"Yeah." She stopped walking and turned to face him. "Why did you choose today to ask me out?" she asked.

He looked up. "It's a sunny day." Then he shrugged. "I don't know."

"I was wondering if it was something I was wearing." She gestured to her red plaid blouse, her gray kilt skirt—her little schoolgirl's outfit, as he liked to think of it. She leaned her head slightly to one side and lifted the end of her long brown hair, playing with it. "Or if it was something else?" she asked.

He looked her straight in the eye, something he had not done in a long time. "It wasn't your clothes," he said.

"Darn."

"Shelly?"

"That means I can't just put on this outfit the next time I want you to ask me out. I won't know what to do." She laughed at his perplexed expression and playfully shoved him away. "What I'm saying, Marvin, is, don't take so long next time."

It was a wonderful life.

======== **CHAPTER 2**

Marvin left the campus at lunch—he didn't know if Shelly turned invisible during that time slot or not. For him to leave halfway through the school day was not unusual. Like many seniors, he had only four periods. He swung his leg over his bike in the parking lot, fastened on his helmet, and sped away from school. He was feeling euphoric about his date with Shelly that night, and whenever he felt strong emotions, good or bad, he drove fast.

He loved his bike because he loved the sensation of speed. The wind on his face, the vibration of the road beneath him, the roar of the engine in his ears—these sensations did more for him than walking a dog on a beach ever would. Yet he still liked to go for walks around the lake, especially late at night when everybody was asleep, when he needed the quiet to think. It seemed his stories came easier when he was surrounded by darkness.

Marvin had a post office box. All his correspondence with his editor and agent passed through this box. His manuscripts, like those of all authors, went through several stages before they were printed in book form: editing, line editing, copy editing, galleys, pages—each step hopefully improving upon what had originally been written. He was, therefore, constantly receiving and sending mail to New York City, where both his publisher and agent were located. On top of that he got five hundred fan letters a week—not a lot by pop rock or TV star standards, but a ton considering that he was a celebrity whom no one had ever seen. All this fan mail was sent to his editor who forwarded it to the P.O. box that his own mother didn't know about.

She didn't even know that he was Mack Slate.

Marvin headed for the post office after leaving school. He hadn't picked up his mail in a few days, and if he didn't get it regularly, his P.O. box would overflow. He was surprised when he walked into the post office, helmet in hand, to find his little sister, Ann, already digging into his envelopes.

"What are you doing here?" he asked, happy to see her. His sister was the closest person to him in the world. She was the only one who knew Mack Slate's true identity. She was only eleven, six years his junior, but already strikingly beautiful. She had amazing green eyes—they were definitely green, she assured him, not hazel—and the face of an angel. Even Shelly, for all her fine features, could not have competed with his sister in a beauty contest. She was also a brilliant child. Both his agent and editor would have been shocked to know an eleven-year-old kid was his only sounding board for his stories. Yet it was not as if Ann gave him ideas so much that she had an uncanny knack of knowing which of his ideas should be discarded.

Ann loved his books, perhaps more than he did. But sometimes she made fun of how he was obsessed with the "dark side." Because so often young girls similar to herself died in his stories, she had once accused him of writing "dead sister" books. He didn't believe the accusation was fair, but as a morbid tribute to her and her help he had begun to make *Ann* the middle name of each of his female victims. It was curious—not a single one of his fans had ever noticed that small fact. The Silver Lake series was the first time he had named the central victim after his sister, which surprisingly pleased her.

"I didn't go to school," Ann said. His box was on the bottom row. Ann jerked upright at his approach and dropped a couple of manila envelopes onto the floor. His editor generally stuffed his fan mail into oversize envelopes before mailing it to him.

"So you thought you'd come by and steal my mail?" he asked, actually pleased she was going to the trouble to get it for him.

"I was bored," Ann said. "I wanted to read the latest batch of teenage girls gushing over you."

"Does it inspire you?" he asked, helping her pick up the mail. Ann had the tiniest hands. Everything about her was small and cute.

"It makes me jealous," she said.

"Really?"

"Just kidding." She stuffed the mail in the green knapsack on her back. She liked to carry it. She was proud of his success. It killed her that she couldn't tell her friends at school about her famous brother.

"Why aren't you at school?" he asked.

"I'm supposed to be sick."

"Are you sick?" he asked.

She giggled. "Of course not. I'm just lazy."

"Did you ride your bike all the way down here?"

"Yes."

Home was two miles away. "Then you're not all that lazy," he said. They finished collecting the mail and walked toward the exit, or he walked and Ann skipped. "How's Mom doing?" he asked reluctantly.

Ann stopped skipping. "She's having a bad day."

A bad day meant she had gotten drunk before noon. Marvin sighed. "I don't know what we're going to do with her," he said.

Ann took his hand. "Do we have to do anything with her?"

The poor girl. She had two alcoholic parents. He thought God would have been satisfied to give her one. But that was one thing writing had taught Marvin about God—for when he wrote, he got to play God—The Man Upstairs was capable of anything.

It was a fantasy of Ann's that when her big brother left home, which he planned to do after he graduated from high school, he'd take her with him. It wasn't that she didn't love her mother, or her father for that matter, whom thankfully she seldom saw. It was just that her parents' problems were too overwhelming for an eleven-year-old girl.

It was primarily because his parents were dysfunctional that Marvin hid his Mack Slate identity. He was two months short of his eighteenth birthday. Until he was eighteen, either one of his parents could seize control of his money, which was approaching the two-million-dollar mark. He kept his money in an ordinary NOW account that he had opened with his mother's help on his thirteenth birthday. But it was an account, he was sure, his mother no longer remembered. He wasn't as worried about her, though, as he was about his dad, who would squander every penny Marvin had made. His dad was not a happy drinker, and he gambled as well as drank. Marvin sometimes thought that if he wrote his dad into a book, the man would come across as unbelievable.

Except to kids who had alcoholic parents.

"We'll have to do something for Mom one of these days," Marvin told Ann, squeezing her hand. "But not today." He messed up her dark hair, which she wore short. "Don't worry about it. Give me your best little Annie smile."

She jerked her hand away and slapped him. "Don't call me Annie! I hate that name, Mr. Slate!"

He laughed. "Shh! Don't call me that name, not here. I'm sorry. Who do you want to be today?" Ann liked to be different fictional characters, sometimes from movies, usually from books. Sometimes a name would stay with her a month, and during that time she would walk around as if she were the character.

"Arwen," she said without hesitation.

"Who?"

"The Elven princess in *The Lord of the Rings,*" she said. "You remember, she married Aragon."

"Of course. So what does she do that I can look forward to?"

Ann's eyes were round as she looked up at him. "She can work magic."

Marvin couldn't help but be warmed by those magic eyes. "I'm sure she can."

They rode home together, side by side. Ann was in a chatty mood, but had to yell over the engine noise. She explained how she had faked a fever so she could watch an R-rated show on cable before their mom got out of bed for the second time. Mrs. Summer usually got up to see them off to school and then reappeared about noon for a pot of coffee and a pack of cigarettes. They lived on their father's child support and the money Marvin brought in from doing ghostwriting for local newspaper reporters—the latter, of course, being a complete fabrication. All those hours he spent writing in his room, his mother thought he was fine-tuning a few lousy articles for throwaway newspapers. His dad was so inconsistent with his payments—his mother drinking away most of what he did send—that they would have been out on the street if Marvin hadn't been chipping in money for the last three years. In fact, his mother was so stoned most of the time she didn't realize that he was paying ninety percent of their upkeep. He didn't mind. He would have given both his parents every cent he had if it would have cured their disease. But he was beginning to believe they would never get better, and that caused him great sorrow.

Their mom was smoking a cigarette and watching TV when they got home. There was no visible sign of liquor because she never drank in front of them. Marvin could count the number of times on the fingers of both hands that he had seen her lift alcohol to her lips. But the vodka bottles that passed through her bedroom were evidence, and so was the damage to her once beautiful face. Just looking at his mom ruined much of the good feeling he had got from asking Shelly out and riding home with Ann. Oh, she was still an attractive woman. Not surprisingly, she looked like an older version of Ann. Her mouth was even wider than Ann's, and she had an excellent figure. It was in her green eyes the damage was most clearly recorded. There was nothing in them—no emotion, no thought—the worst of all things. Sometimes when he spoke to his mother he imagined that he was talking to an animated corpse. He prayed it didn't come to that. The doctor said that already two-thirds of her liver was shot.

Still, he didn't know why she drank. He didn't know why his father did. It wasn't as if he and Ann had driven them to it.

"Hi," he said, coming around to give her a hug and a kiss. She was watching a video of an old Clark Gable movie. Humphrey Bogart, Grace Kelly, Fred Astaire, Greta Garbo—all her favorites.

She seldom watched anyone who wasn't from the black-and-white era, which was curious because she wasn't that old. But she loved those good old days when men were noble and women never seemed to age.

"Hello, Marvin," she said, giving him a brief dry kiss. "How was school?"

"Glorious," he said. "I got a B on my English paper—on that frog story I told you about."

She took a drag on her cigarette, her eyes returning to the TV screen. "Don't you study frogs in biology?"

"This wasn't exactly a scientific paper," he said.

"Hello, Mom," Ann chimed in.

"Hello," her mother replied, reaching for the remote control. She raised the volume a couple of notches without even looking over at Ann. He had always been her favorite, which annoyed both of them. "Have you done your chores?" Mom asked.

"Yes, Mom, I did them before I went to school," Ann said, and of course it was an absurd lie. But their mom didn't even register the fact, not even when Ann had pretended to be sick that morning. Marvin could smell the alcohol in the air—between six and eight ounces of eighty-proof vodka in her system. His nose had become sensitive over the years.

"That's nice," their mom said.

"I'm going to go work in my room," Marvin said.

"OK," she said.

"I'm going to help him," Ann added.

"Finish your chores first."

His room was his sanctuary. Although they lived

on a conservative budget, their house was spacious, and the three bedrooms upstairs were each large enough to accommodate their private lives. For all his wealth Marvin had bought himself very few luxuries, partly because he didn't want to alert people to the fact of his money, but also because he just didn't care that much about stuff. But he did have an excellent stereo system and almost a thousand CDs. He had a hard time writing unless he had loud music on, which was weird because when he had started to write—when he was thirteen—he had found it impossible to compose a paragraph without complete silence. He didn't really hear the music when he was working, even with headphones on. One of his favorite songs would come on and he would make a mental note to enjoy it while he was writing, but then a few minutes later he'd realize the song was finished and he hadn't heard a word of it. He believed the music helped by distracting his conscious mind, while not fully taking it away from his work. In other words, he needed his attention on what he was doing, but he also needed to be on automatic to write his best stuff. It was the *flow* that mattered, the power of the story coming through. He honestly felt the entire thinking process was overrated when it came to writing. When he sat and tried to construct a provocative paragraph it inevitably came out stilted and strained.

"Can we read your mail now?" Ann asked, plopping down on his bed and removing her backpack. She dumped the letters onto his bedspread.

"Sure," Marvin said. He sat at his desk and flipped on his computer. It was doubtful he was going to get any work done in the next few hours, what with his chronic writer's block and his upcoming date with Shelly, but sometimes just turning on the word processor helped. When he had started writing he did it all in longhand, resisting getting a word processor because he couldn't type. But his agent had finally talked him into buying a computer, and when he wrote his next novel in a month he was sold on the thing. He could write incredibly fast when he had to. Once, under the pressure of a deadline, he had written an entire book in eleven days.

"I wonder if any of the letters will ask where you get your ideas," Ann said, plucking an envelope from the pile. Marvin reached over and picked up a handful of letters and set them in his lap. Ann was being sarcastic with her comment. Half the mail he received asked where he got his ideas, as if it were a question he could answer.

"I hope there are some pictures," Marvin said. Often his fans sent him photographs of themselves. Occasionally there was even a nude picture, which made him nervous—though he had never thrown any of them away. Ann looked at him in disgust. She knew too much about him he sometimes thought.

"How gross," Ann said. She opened the letter in her hand. "Do you want me to read it to you?"

"Don't bother, I'll get to it." He read all the mail he got and suffered continuous guilt that he was able to answer so little of it. He had once calculated that if he answered each letter he received, he would have to give up both writing and sleeping.

But occasionally he would scribble a note in response—if a particular letter had touched him or if the fan was sick or something.

Marvin reached down for a letter in his lap. He used the letter opener on his desk to open the envelope. It was a fairly standard fan letter.

Dear Mr. Slate,

I just wanted to tell you that you are the most awesome writer in the whole world. I have read every one of your books. I can't believe how good they are! When I'm reading them I feel like I'm right there doing all the things the characters are doing. Sometimes I get so scared while reading one of your stories that I have to sleep with the lights on. You always keep me in suspense right up until the last page. You are simply the greatest!

My name is Nancy Berg and I live in a small town in Iowa. I'm sixteen years old and a junior in high school. I have two older brothers, a dog named Shirley, and bad asthma. My hobbies include playing piano, theater, and reading your books. My goal is to someday be a writer like you. You are a great inspiration to me.

I was wondering if I could ask you some questions. Here they are.

1. Where do you get your ideas?

2. How old are you?

3. Are you married?

4. How long does it usually take you to write a book?

5. How much money do you make?

6. Are any of the characters in your books based on real people?

Right now I'm reading your The Mystery of Silver Lake *series. It's the best! I'm dying to know who killed Ann McGaffer. I can hardly wait for the last book.*

Well, I've got to go. Hope to hear from you soon.

Your #1 Fan,
Nancy

"Was it your number one fan?" Ann asked.

"Yeah, it was a nice letter," Marvin said, setting it down. He reached for another. "How was yours?"

"It was also from your number one fan," Ann said, and giggled. The letters cracked her up, but Marvin viewed them differently. It was hard to take seriously the adoration heaped upon him in the letters, especially when he was treated so normally in his everyday life. But he also realized that he must have deeply affected the people who wrote or they wouldn't go to the trouble of telling him how much his work meant to them.

The next letter had no nude pictures enclosed. It didn't need them.

Dear Mr. Slate,

I love your books. I love you. I feel like I know you. I see you in your work—a part here, a piece there. I have this fantasy about you—that you are really God and we are all just characters in your stories. Or that maybe you're the devil,

*and that you are going to lead us into wicked
sin. I fantasize about these things all the time.*

*I had this dream about you last night. I'm a
senior in high school and in gym we still have to
take showers. In my dream I was alone in the
showers, naked, and you came walking in wearing a black tux. At first I was shy, even when you
told me who you were because I didn't believe
that you were the real Mack Slate. But then you
started kissing me under the warm shower, and
your hands were all over my body, and I knew it
was you. You were like the devil 'cause you were
so forceful, but it was so good, the sex, that you
were like God as well.*

You can see that I'm a real big fan.

*I want you to do me a favor. I want you to
write me back and give me your phone number.
I want you to give me directions to your house. I
want you to fly me to your front doorstep. I want
a part of you, a piece of you, and in return I'm
going to give you all of me. I think it will be
sweet. Don't keep me waiting long.*

*Love you,
Becky*

Mack casually set the letter aside. Becky had not
given him her phone number, but he could probably get it from Information. She'd be fun to talk to
on the phone. Sometimes, when he was lonely, he'd
call up girls who had written him provocative
letters, especially late at night. He'd had a few
steamy conversations in the last year. Just because
he wrote intriguing books, they all thought he had

special insight into what made them tick. They also assumed he must be fantastically sexy. Of course when he talked to them he did nothing to destroy their illusions.

He sometimes wondered if they had known he was only in high school would they have worshiped him so?

Ann raised an eyebrow as he set the letter aside. "A girl who wants to take off her clothes for you?" she asked.

"Not at all." He opened his desk drawer and put the letter inside. "It's from the mother of a teenage girl who's dying of leukemia."

"Can I read it?" Ann asked.

"You wouldn't want to. It's very depressing."

Ann nodded. "I bet you this poor sick girl's last wish is to kiss the great Mack Slate."

Marvin had to laugh. Ann could see right through him. "She believes it will cure her," he said.

He was almost through his pile of envelopes when he came across a fan letter that had been mailed from Sesa to his publisher in New York. He could tell by the Sesa postmark—there was no return address. He was surprised. Sesa was a small town of only ten thousand. It was true he got letters from all over America—the whole world for that matter—but even with the volume of mail he received, the odds against his getting a letter from his hometown were slim. He fingered the letter thoughtfully before opening it.

"What's the matter?" Ann asked, looking up.

"Someone from Sesa sent this."

"What does it say?"

"I don't know."

Ann was intrigued. "Open it. Read it."

Marvin tore open the envelope. The note was only one sentence long, typed on clean white paper in capital letters.

I KNOW WHO YOU ARE.

"I know who you are," Marvin whispered aloud, and he felt his heart skip a beat. Ann quickly went over and knelt beside him. She plucked the letter from his hand and studied it.

"It's probably just a crank letter," she said after a moment. "If they knew who you were they would have called you by your real name."

"I disagree," Marvin said. "This is the first letter I've ever received that said this—and this one was mailed from right here. That's too much of a coincidence. The person must know who I am."

"But how?"

Marvin was troubled. "I don't know. Maybe someone noticed me at the post office collecting my mail and saw the name on an envelope. Ben wouldn't have told anybody." Ben Friar was his agent. For tax reasons, it was necessary that Ben knew his true identity and his Social Security number. But even Ben didn't know he was still in high school. They had only talked on the phone. His own editor believed his real name was Mack Slate.

"Are you sure?" Ann asked.

"I can always ask him." Marvin took back the letter and studied it. The note had been typed with an old-fashioned typewriter, but other than that there were no clues to the identity of the sender.

I know who you are.

The message was simple enough. Yet, because of its very vagueness, it carried with it an underlying threat, Marvin thought.

"What are you going to do?" Ann asked, worried. She lived in fear that their father might take everything Marvin had earned to punish them for keeping their secret from him.

"There isn't anything I can do," Marvin replied. The more he thought about it, the more likely it seemed that his identity had been uncovered at the post office. It was even possible an employee there had leaked the information. He briefly considered checking out the idea, but decided that would only draw more attention to himself.

What troubled him most was *why* someone would send him such a letter. Perhaps the person recognized his strong desire to remain anonymous and was planning to blackmail him. He wouldn't be surprised if he received another letter soon. But he was only concerned, not anxious. Chances were the unknown sender was just trying to give him the creeps. Blackmail was a dangerous game to play, and the person who sent the letter must know that.

"Should you go to the police?" Ann asked.

Marvin laughed and messed up her hair. "No. It's probably just a letter from another adoring fan. Who knows? You might be right. The person who sent it might not even know my real name—it was sent to Mack Slate."

Right then the phone rang. Marvin reached for it.

41

It was his editor—Pat Winchell. She was his bene-factor. She was the first person, outside of his agent, to recognize his talent and buy one of his books. Even though he was enjoying tremendous success now, he had gone through a hard year of rejections before Pat picked up one of his novels. He could remember with complete clarity the day his agent had called him with the news. He had just returned home from school and was lying on his bed staring at the ceiling and wondering if he was going to have to live in Sesa the rest of his life with his zombie mother and nasty father. Then the phone had rung. Congratulations! It was a good thing he was lying down. He had been given only a paltry advance—five thousand dollars—and the minimum royalty rate, but it had been the happiest day of his life. His book was going to be in print! People were going to walk into bookstores and pick it up and buy it! That prospect alone was enough to have him walking on clouds for days. It was one of those thrills that he doubted he would ever reexperience.

Pat was a senior editor at the largest publisher in the world. She was always nice to him, but the pressure on her—and consequently on him as her biggest author—was immense. She wanted a mas-terpiece every time, and she wanted it on time. The final installment of the Silver Lake series was four months overdue.

"How are you doing, Mack?" Pat asked.

"Great. How are you?"

"I'm worried about your book. Are you almost done?"

"Getting there. It just needs a little fine-tuning."

A note of desperation entered her voice. "Can you please tell me when I can see it? We have only three months to publication. You know this timetable is unheard of, Mack."

He sighed. "I know."

"You didn't answer my question. When can I see it? If we wait any longer we'll have to push back the pub date, and the chains will have to be notified, and you'll lose the momentum you've built for yourself with your other books."

"I'm on the last chapter," he said.

She paused. She was a high-strung woman and often forgetful, but she was shrewd. She had discovered him, after all. She probably knew he was lying, only she couldn't imagine to what extent.

"What is the absolute longest it will take you to get it to me?" she asked finally.

Marvin considered. "Ten days."

She wasn't happy. He didn't have the heart to tell her how happy she should have been about ten days. "That long?" she said.

"That would be the maximum," he said smoothly. It would be the minimum—if he started writing right now and didn't sleep for ten days. But he couldn't start anything right now because he didn't know where he or the book was heading. Besides, he had to go out with Shelly tonight. Dear Shelly—he would have to put her in a book someday. He added, "It's going to be a fantastic book, Pat. The best of them all."

He had her now. Besides being his editor, she was his fan, and that made a big difference. Right from the beginning she had pushed him at the publishing house. A note of delight entered her voice. "Does it have a shocking ending?" she asked.

"Oh, yeah. You won't believe it. It's unimaginable."

"Is there any way at all that you can get it in earlier than ten days?" Pat asked.

"It's possible. I'll see what I can do. I'm working right now. I should probably go."

"If you're working, I'll let you go. Burn the midnight oil if you have to, Mack, but get me that book."

"I understand." They exchanged goodbyes and he set down the phone. Ann was staring at him.

"Is Pat worried?" Ann asked.

"Not as worried as she should be."

"What are you going to do?"

Marvin glanced at his computer screen—his blank computer screen. "I'll start writing," he said.

"When?"

"Tomorrow." He stood and stretched. "I'm going out tonight. Guess who with?"

Ann did not look happy. "Shelly Quade."

"Yeah. Aren't you happy for me?"

Ann lowered her head. "You should stay home and write."

Her reaction surprised him. A trace of annoyance entered his voice. "How? I don't know what to write."

Ann looked up sharply. "And you think Shelly's going to help you?"

"What's gotten into you? What's wrong with Shelly?"

"You went out with her. You should know what's wrong with her."

"What's that supposed to mean?" he asked.

Ann stood and walked to the door. "It doesn't matter what I say or think. I'm just a kid." She opened the door and left. He stared after her, dumbfounded. He had never known Ann disliked Shelly. Ann had listened to him talk about her, but he had only said positive things. As far as he knew the two had never met.

Marvin turned back to his computer, sat there for a while doing absolutely nothing, then turned it off. He checked his watch—two-thirty. He had three and a half hours to kill before he picked up Shelly. He remembered he had promised her he'd try to find a car. He decided to ask his mother just before he left if he could borrow hers. There was no use in giving her time to think about something, because during that time she would kill the brain cells that held the information she was supposed to be contemplating.

Marvin decided to go for a walk. He put on his leather jacket. The days were getting cooler. Tonight, he heard, was supposed to be below freezing.

He didn't see his mother or Ann as he left the house. He got on his bike and rode down to Sesa Lake. Along the shore was dying grass, with an occasional spruce tree, except at the west end of the lake where the hills collided with the water to form the cliff Harry had jumped off; there the ground was laced with crunchy orange gravel. Marvin had the place to himself. The day was sunny but the water was a dull gray, covered with listless ripples, cold and uninviting. Marvin wondered if it was just his eyes. When he was young he used to have nightmares about the lake. He would dream that he was walking along the shore late at night, when suddenly he would hear loud splashing coming from the middle of the lake, a place he couldn't see in the dark. He would try to run away but would encounter an invisible barrier that would stop him from fleeing. He was only allowed to run along the shore. The splashing would grow louder and louder, and he would just know that whatever was emerging from the depths was going to eat him— every little boy's worst fear. But then, when the monster was about to pounce, there would be a flash of bright red light, and Marvin would wake up facedown on the ground and it would be daytime. Only he would still be dreaming because he would wake up beside the lake—what was left of it. All the water would be drained from the lake, and the dry bed would be littered with dozens of human skeletons, their bones a bleached white under a haunted gray sky.

It was a dream he had many times as a boy.

Was it any wonder he had set the body of the main victim of his series floating facedown in a lake? Where do you get your ideas, Mr. Slate? Well, my dear, some of them come from a place I'd rather not revisit.

My main victim?

He had yet to decide whether he was going to kill anybody else in the final book. He didn't want to.

He had begun to develop an affection for his characters, even the evil ones.

Marvin walked aimlessly around the lake, but no fresh inspiration came to him. He had circumvented the lopsided body of water twice when it began to get dark. It was time to get home and dress for his date.

CHAPTER 3

Marvin didn't get to borrow his mother's car. It turned out it was broken. She asked him to call and have it towed to the shop when he asked if he could borrow it. He hoped Shelly was able to get ahold of a car or they'd have a cold night on the road.

Shelly answered the door when he knocked. She was dressed simply in blue corduroy jeans and a shiny yellow blouse. She had her hair tied back in twin ponytails, with bright yellow ribbons. Her smile lit him up. Yet it was a casual smile. Shelly was usually in control of most situations.

"Do we have a car?" she asked.

He looked downcast. "Do we?" he asked.

She gave an exaggerated sigh. "I guess I should get my warmest jacket."

"Your parents won't let you borrow their car?"

"They're away for the weekend." She gestured for him to enter and turned in the direction of her bedroom. "Do we know what we're doing?"

We are going to have sex. Eat dinner. Have sex. Go to the movies. And have sex.

"I thought maybe we could go for dinner and a movie," Marvin suggested, watching her walk away. She had a cute butt, Shelly did.

"Are we staying in Sesa?" she called from her room. He had been in there twice, a year ago. He had even lain on her bed and kissed her. The Quades had a huge house, with a Jacuzzi on the back porch.

"I thought maybe we'd go to Pella," he called back. Pella was a neighboring town, about twenty miles distant, maybe four times larger than Sesa. There the selection of movie theaters and restaurants was far better. "When I thought we had a car."

Shelly reappeared with a blue ski jacket. "I knew you weren't going to get a car. That's why I tied my hair back."

"I tried, honestly."

She shook her head. "You boys and your bikes." She slipped into her jacket. "Pella's fine. I need the cold wind on my face. It brings out the color in my cheeks."

"You're always colorful," Marvin said. He meant it.

She smiled, her sweet Shelly smile, which was filled with all good things. "And you always say the right thing," she replied.

* * *

They ate at a restaurant called the Big Fish. Surprisingly, neither had seafood. Shelly ordered turkey and rice and Marvin had a chicken sandwich and fries. Their waitress was disappointed they wouldn't try the lobster. Marvin turned it down because he had no taste for it, but Shelly confessed after ordering that she loved lobster, but hadn't wanted to break him. He told her to enjoy herself. Money was no problem.

Their food came and they ate hungrily. The cold wind had stimulated both their appetites. The conversation flowed easily. Marvin could be quite the talker—when he wasn't trying to ask somebody out. Shelly told him about her plans to be a doctor one day. She wanted to specialize in plastic surgery—a curious specialty, he thought, for a pretty girl. But she said she dreamed of making everyone beautiful. She asked about his ambition to be a writer. He mumbled something about how hard it was to get published, but she was keen on the subject and really wanted him to pursue it.

They went to a movie. It was boring, and because it was warm inside the theater, in contrast to the cold outside, Marvin dozed off. It was embarrassing. When Shelly shook him awake she told him he'd been snoring. His biggest night in a long time and he fell asleep. Oh, well, Shelly thought it was funny.

Around eleven o'clock they started back toward Sesa.

Between the two towns stretched the Pella River, a narrow but deep and strong river that fed directly into Lake Sesa. The bridge that crossed the river was an antique collection of old rusted steel support beams with creaking boards laid crosswise for the floor. Twenty years earlier it had been used as a train bridge. The river ran between two low ranges of grass-covered hills, one on the Pella side, the other on the Sesa. It was fun, particularly on a bike, to come flying over either of the hills and race down toward the bridge. On many occasions Marvin had crossed the bridge doing close to a hundred. That night, with Shelly hugging his waist, he was doing better than seventy when she called out for him to stop.

"Why?" he shouted over the roar of the wind. He had a scarf wrapped around his face, and had his glasses on; nevertheless his cheeks and eyeballs were ready to freeze. Being the cool dude that he was he had volunteered his helmet to Shelly.

"I want to look at the river!" she shouted.

"It's cold!"

"I know it's cold! I still want to stop and look!"

He eased up on the throttle and let the bike slow down in the middle of the bridge. He pulled over to the side. Shelly jumped off the back before they came to a complete stop. Below them they could hear the loud roar of the river. The wind was brisk. Marvin scanned in both directions along the road. If a car approached, they would see its lights from far off. He killed the engine and climbed off the bike. Shelly had already removed her helmet and set it on the wooden floor of the bridge.

"What are we doing?" he asked. He could hardly see her face in the black. She rubbed her gloved hands together and bounced on her toes.

"I love this spot," she said. "I just wanted to see it."

"You should have waited for a moonlit night." Marvin glanced at the rusted-through rails. He knew how frail they were. "If we're not careful, we could fall in."

As if to challenge his last remark, Shelly stepped right up to the rail and leaned over and looked down. The water was a hundred fifty feet below. "We'd float all the way to Lake Sesa," she said.

"Careful," Marvin said. He reached out and grabbed the back of her jacket. She turned to the side and pulled him closer. Yet she continued to stare down into the foaming water. Marvin figured there must have been rain farther upstream; the river was a regular torrent. He added, "You'd be dead by the time you got there."

She looked over at him, her ponytails flapping in the breeze. "You'd drown?" she asked.

"You'd drown and you'd die from hypothermia. I don't know which would happen first." He caught himself before elaborating further. The topic of Harry's suicide had not come up all evening and he didn't want it to. Shelly continued to watch him.

"Do you know a lot about stuff like that?" she asked.

He was something of an expert when it came to the different ways a person could die—common among mystery writers. But he shrugged at her question. "I know a few things," he said.

She sat down suddenly, sticking her legs in the spaces between the rusted rails so that her feet were dangling, making him more nervous. "You can feel the spray of the river on your face," she said, pulling off her gloves and rubbing her cheeks.

"You can feel it as you *drive* by." Marvin reluctantly sat beside her. He could do without ice-cold spray on his face when he was already shivering. Perhaps, though, Shelly read his mind, for she leaned over and took his arm in hers and drew him to her side. He had accidentally sat on a piece of rope, and had to reach down to pull it aside.

"I enjoyed the movie," she said.

"Did I?"

She laughed. "Yeah, you looked like it brought you peace of mind. You know most girls would have taken your falling asleep as a personal insult."

"But not this girl?"

"This girl is easy to please."

"Is that true?" he asked and was curious because Shelly had always struck him as someone who wouldn't settle for anything but the best in life. That was not to say she was a snob—rather, she wanted the most she could get out of her short time on earth. Shelly folded her fingers around his.

"I only want love," she replied, and her voice was sad. She turned once more to look down into the water. It seemed to hold a hypnotic fascination for her.

"What about being a plastic surgeon?"

She smiled faintly at his question. "To make the whole world beautiful," she muttered. She sat there silently for a few moments, with her head bowed, and then abruptly raised it. Her voice regained its earlier energy. "What would you like to do now more than anything in the world?" she asked.

Sit naked in your Jacuzzi with you.

"Get warm," he said.

She stood. "Let's go get in my Jacuzzi. Would you like that?"

He got up. "Sure," he said nonchalantly.

God bless parents who went away for the weekend, Marvin thought as he reentered Shelly's house. She was ahead of him, pulling off her coat, striding into her bedroom.

"Would you like some coffee?" she called back.

"Do you keep it in your chest of drawers?"

"What?" She was now in her room.

"I'll have some if you're having some!" he called.

She reappeared. She was quick on her feet. "I don't need it. Do you have a bathing suit?"

"Yes, I do. I always keep one in a secret compartment in my motorcycle helmet."

"Good." She paused and there was amusement in her eyes. "I don't have one that will fit you."

He met her gaze. "I don't have one that will fit you."

Shelly smiled. "So we're even." She blushed. "I have three in my bedroom that fit me perfectly."

Marvin felt bold. The entire night had given him confidence. She had made it clear she liked him a lot. "But that's no fair. I have to sit naked in your Jacuzzi while you get to hide behind three bathing suits."

"I was just going to wear one." She added, "Besides, we don't have to go in the Jacuzzi."

He acted indifferent. "All right. Let's not."

She was insulted. "You are so full of it, Mr.

Summer. You are dying to sit naked in my Jacuzzi with me."

"Who said anything about being naked?"

"You did. You said the word first."

"Well, I could keep my underwear on." He added, lying, "Except I don't think I'm wearing any."

She raised a gorgeous Shelly eyebrow. Except he wasn't really concentrating on her eyebrows. He was thinking of—well, he was thinking of many good things that only a few hours ago had seemed out of reach, but which now, miraculously, might be sitting next to him in a few warm minutes.

"I don't think I'm wearing any, either," she said.

"Then that settles that."

She blushed again. "I can't take off my clothes in front of you. I'm too shy."

"I'll look the other way. We'll put bubble bath in the Jacuzzi. I'll gouge out my eyes."

She giggled. "I do have bubble bath." She paused. "All right."

His heart skipped so hard it almost tripped. But it kept beating; he made sure it did. He wouldn't forgive himself if he died right now. "All right," he said.

Marvin got in the Jacuzzi while Shelly ran to the bathroom. The water was very hot, and he wondered if the Quades always kept it at such a high temperature during the winter. Their gas bill must be atrocious.

Shelly reappeared and he quickly crossed his legs, although he doubted she could see much. He had already turned on the jets. She was fully clothed. She had a carton of bubble bath in her hand. She read the label.

"How does lavender heaven sound?" she asked.

"A little fruity."

"Yes, but we know that neither of us is gay." She opened the top and poured the whole thing in the tub.

"Shelly!"

She laughed. "We'll have bubbles up to the ceiling." She tossed the carton aside and began to undo her belt. "Gouge out your eyes, Marvin, I'm going to take off my clothes."

"Can't I just cover them with my hands?"

"So you can peek between your fingers? Yeah, that would be all right." She threw a sponge at him when he flashed a wide-open eyeball between his fingers. "You are not going to see me naked on our first date!"

"This is our sixth date," he protested.

That quieted her. "Turn your head away."

Marvin obeyed. He couldn't believe what a good little boy he was being. He waited until she told him he could look. By then she was in the water, well hidden behind a mountain of pink bubbles.

"It's hot," she said.

"It sure is," Marvin marveled.

She reddened. "You better not tell anyone at school that we did this."

"No one would believe me, Shelly." He reached out with his toe and brushed the side of her invisible calf, which made her jump slightly. He could see her face, her neck, a little more than her neck. But he could not see her breasts. "So what do couples talk about in a hot tub?" he asked.

She picked up a handful of suds and rubbed it along the side of her cheek. Steam wafted through her long brown curls, and it was hard for him to imagine a more beautiful picture.

"Are we a couple, Marvin?" she asked.

"I didn't mean to be presumptuous."

"You're not."

"To answer your question—I don't know." He added, against his better judgment, "Maybe I should ask Triad."

She chewed on that one a moment, watching him. "He's just a friend. And no, I've never sat naked in the Jacuzzi with him."

"I wasn't going to ask that."

"But you were wondering. True?"

He shrugged. "You're perceptive."

She continued to watch him. "But not as perceptive as you." She added, as if expanding on the same idea, "That was a great story this morning. Jackson should have given you an A."

"What did you like about it? Besides its grossness?"

"It was funny. You're funny. That's why I think you'll make a great writer." She played with the bubbles. They were going down slowly. "Did you want to ask me anything else about Triad?"

"Not really. I don't want to spoil the moment."

She smiled. "I thought you'd forgotten about me."

"Because I took so long to ask you out again?"

"Yes," she said.

"It's hard to forget someone when you sit behind them every day—and look at them."

She was interested. "Do you look at me that much?"

"Only when I'm bored."

She splashed him. "You're never sweet without being mean at the same time."

He reached out and grabbed her hands. They were slippery, soft. He hadn't held them in a long time. "School is always boring," he said.

She was touched. "So you watch me all the time?"

He slid around the edge of the Jacuzzi seat, still holding her hands, until he was sitting beside her. He could feel her bare thigh against his, her hip. "I'm never bored when I watch you," he said. He let go of one of her hands and touched her left shoulder. "Can I kiss you?"

She touched his shoulder, the far one, and the bubbles were becoming less an obstacle all the time. "You don't have to ask me twice." She brushed his lips with her fingertips. "You asked me the same thing last November."

He kissed her and she kissed him and their arms went around each other and he felt he was sinking into an ocean of joy, rather than a mere hot tub. He caressed her, he wasn't sure where, and she moaned with pleasure. Or maybe he moaned. It was a big world, he knew, a bigger universe, but in that moment there was only her—nothing else—and yet he had never felt so full. He forgot his fears and his jokes, which with him were two sides of the same coin. As he kissed her his mind went empty, as it did when he raced at high speed on his bike.

But then she tried to pull away, and it took him a few seconds to register that fact. He let go of her with a twinge of embarrassment. "I'm sorry," he said quickly.

She was staring at him with what appeared to be confusion. But then she lowered her eyes and smiled again, yet this smile, too, like the one on the bridge, was somehow sad. "You don't have to be sorry," she said. "I wanted to kiss you, too."

He started to hold her again, but hesitated. She had been shaken to the core, and yet he didn't believe it was his kiss that had done it. It struck him then how little he knew her.

"What else do you want?" he asked.

She looked around and frowned. "We should get out of here. The bubbles are dying." She went to stand. He grabbed her arm.

"Don't you want me to turn around?" he asked.

She thought a moment. "You don't have to."

He watched her get out of the hot tub. She had a wonderful bottom, beautiful breasts. Yet he didn't enjoy the sight of her naked body as much as he would have imagined. There was something on her mind, that was for sure, and it wasn't just him. A few minutes later they were both dressed and he was on the verge of leaving when she grabbed him once more and kissed him hard. But there was a desperation to the way she held on to him. And when she let go and spoke he understood a big part of what was happening.

"Harry didn't commit suicide," she whispered

into his chest, her wet hair hanging over her face. He gripped her shoulders and held her at arm's length.

"What are you talking about?" he asked.

A tear ran over her cheek as she looked at him. "He was murdered."

He was shocked, and he was Mack Slate. Why would a famous mystery writer be surprised to learn what he wrote about really happened? Maybe because he didn't believe in the reality of his work. They were just made-up stories. Or maybe because he believed Shelly was simply emotionally distraught. Yet it was funny how the thought of Ann McGaffer crossed his mind right then.

"Who killed him?" Marvin asked.

Shelly's eyes were big, glassy. "I don't know."

"Then how do you know he was murdered?"

Another tear came, and fell onto the floor. "He wouldn't have killed himself. I know." She grabbed his hand and pressed it to her chest. "I know it in my heart."

He couldn't help it, but her revelation—he didn't know how else to think of it—hurt his feelings. He didn't believe she'd have shed a tear for him after a year's time.

"Why are you telling me this?" he asked.

"Because I want you to help me find his murderer," she said.

"Why me?"

"Because you care." She hugged him. "You just made me feel you care. Will you help me?"

Marvin rested his chin on the top of her head. He

had dreamed of holding her, and now he realized that she had been dreaming of holding a dead guy. But since Harry wasn't there to answer her, he supposed he must.

"I'll help you," he promised.

CHAPTER 4

The next day was Saturday. Marvin woke early and stared at the ceiling for a couple of hours. He was both excited and depressed by his date with Shelly. She liked him more than he had imagined, but she was also more obsessed with Harry than he knew. She had offered no evidence to substantiate her claim that Harry had been murdered, saying that they would talk about it today at noon. Marvin doubted she'd have anything significant to add to the case. For an author of mysteries, Marvin was remarkably cynical when it came to believing in hidden plots and secret agendas.

He was worried, not about Harry, but about his book. It was the type of anxiety that continued to grow even when he wasn't thinking about it. The deadline would suddenly flash in his mind and he would feel a little more sick to his stomach than he had the previous time he had remembered what he had to get done. But how could he start? He still hadn't a clue in which direction to go. He considered calling his editor and telling her he was stuck. But then she'd know he had been lying all along, and his career would suffer a serious setback—just as it was beginning.

Marvin finally crawled out of bed and got dressed. He had three hours to kill till noon. He decided he might as well go to the post office to see if he had any more mail. He was procrastinating and he knew it, but such was the daily life of a writer. He was outside, climbing on his bike, when Ann came riding up on hers. She wanted to go with him.

"I don't want you to ride on the back," he said.

"Go slow, we won't crash," she said.

"No. I'll go slow so that you can ride beside me, on your bike." He had always been paranoid about Ann riding on the back of his motorcycle, unnaturally so. He wasn't sure as to the source of it, other than that he knew how bad a wipeout could be on a motorcycle.

Ann relented and they drove to the post office. Along the way she asked him how his date with Shelly had gone, but he could tell she was still unhappy about the relationship and he didn't say much.

He had only one letter in his mailbox. It was a fan letter, addressed to Mack Slate. This one had not been forwarded to him from his publisher. Someone had stuffed it into the mailbox. He tore it open. As before the message was short, typed on a single white page in capital letters.

SHE DOESN'T LOVE YOU
THE WAY YOU THINK SHE DOES.

"What the hell," he whispered. Ann pulled the letter from his hand and read it.

"Who's *she?*" Ann asked.

"The letter must be referring to Shelly."

Ann wrinkled her nose. "You love Shelly?"

Marvin cleared his throat. "The letter is not talking about my love for Shelly, or my lack of love. It's talking about hers."

"Do you think she loves you?" Ann asked.

Marvin forced a chuckle. "No. We hardly know each other." Yet the message had hit him hard in the gut. Now he was not so much asking himself who was sending the letters as he was wondering whether the person was right.

"What's wrong?" Ann asked.

"What do you mean, what's wrong? Someone knows who I am."

"You said that it wasn't the end of the world if someone did."

"Yeah," he said. "But now they're getting personal."

"But you just said you hardly know Shelly."

"I didn't say that," he said.

"Yes, you did."

Marvin knelt beside his sister. "Why don't you like Shelly?"

She looked at the ground. "I told you why."

"Because she dumped me before?"

"That's one reason."

"What's another?"

Ann looked him straight in the eye. "I just don't like her."

"Why not?"

"I just don't."

Marvin took the letter back and checked the postmark. It had been mailed the day before. "There's a sequence to these letters," he said. "I had to receive the other one first for this one to make sense to me. The person who sent it knows that."

"What does that mean?" Ann asked.

"It means we were being watched yesterday when we picked up the mail. Because I could have got my fan mail today, or Monday for that matter. Yet the person who's sending these letters knew I already had that first one. Only then did he or she put this one in my box." He paused and scanned the area. They were alone in their corner of the post office. Yet the building had many windows and someone down the street could have been observing them this very instant if he had a pair of binoculars. Ann looked around with him, worried.

"What are we going to do?" she asked.

"There's nothing we can do. If this person wants something from us, he'll make it clear soon. Until then we'll wait."

"Are you scared?" Ann asked.

"No." He picked her up as he stood back up and

gave her a hug. "There's nothing to be scared of. This isn't one of my books, you know. No one's going to try to kill me."

Ann hugged him back. "But what if someone tries to kill me?" she asked.

Even though Marvin had told his sister there was nothing to do he called his agent, Ben Friar, as soon as he got home. He had met Ben three years earlier through the mail, and now they talked regularly on the phone. He could hardly remember what age he had told Ben he was—twenty-eight or twenty-nine. He had plucked Ben's name, along with four others, out of *Writer's Market*. He knew it would be difficult to get an agent without a published book under his belt, but he also knew it would be next to impossible to get a book published without an agent. He had already submitted his work to dozens of publishers and got nothing but form letters in response. Thanks, but no thanks. It was one of those catch-22s that made launching a career as a world-famous writer so terribly difficult.

Marvin had sent each of the agents a couple of sample chapters and an outline of a novel called *The Wishing Web*—a story about an apprentice sorcerer who visits a high school and causes all kinds of wicked fun. Ben was the only one who wrote him back. He wanted to see the entire manuscript, which Marvin promptly mailed overnight express to him. Marvin could remember waiting hysterically for Ben's response, and Ben did keep him waiting—a big ten weeks. But Ben's letter, when it came, was enthusiastic. He believed he could place the manuscript, he said, while suggesting a few minor changes in the story structure and the character descriptions, which Marvin was happy to make.

Then came a second period of waiting while most of the New York publishing houses proceeded to bounce the book. The editors of teen fiction didn't like it, they said, because it was too *sophisticated*. That very word was in five rejection slips Ben received. Marvin could not believe it, nor could Ben. In essence the editors were saying that teenagers were not smart enough to read an intelligent plot. And it was true that, as far as complexity was concerned, his book was more akin to an adult novel. But it was Marvin's belief that most teen books were written down to kids, and that was why most of his friends had gone from reading young adult stuff to adult stuff. But then Ben had lunch with Pat, and she reviewed the book and made an offer on it because she enjoyed reading it.

The Wishing Web went on to be a huge bestseller.

Marvin dialed Ben's number from memory. Ben was on another line but got rid of his other caller. Ben was always on another line. He said he slept with a phone tied to the side of his head. He wanted to know how the book was doing.

"Fine," Marvin said without enthusiasm.

Ben knew him well. "Have you started on it yet?"

"No."

"You're kidding me, aren't you?"

"Well . . ."

"Marvin! That book is the single most in-demand book in the history of teen publishing. It's already four months late."

"I am aware of these facts."

"What's wrong?"

"I don't know who killed Ann McGaffer."

"You told me you did."

"I thought I knew, but I don't. I can't start on the book until I do."

"Have the jealous boyfriend be the murderer. Have the slimy brother. It doesn't matter who did it. It's how you tell it. You cannot tell a bad story. Marvin, just start writing."

"I will. Soon. I'll start today. I can do it. I've been late before. I always pull it off; you know that."

Ben hesitated, perhaps sensing the strain he was under. "I'm sure you'll do just fine." He lightened his tone. "I've got some good news for you. Universal Studios has agreed to let you write the screenplay for *The Wishing Web.*"

Marvin felt a wave of pleasure. Hollywood was funny. Filmmakers were only too happy to buy an author's book, but heaven forbid they let the author write the script for the movie. Marvin believed that was why there were so many bad movies made from great books. He had been insisting for months that he write the screenplay.

"How much are they going to pay me?" Marvin asked.

"A lot. I'm still negotiating with them. But they want you to fly down to meet with them—the director, the producer. This will be within the next month. I'd be happy to meet you in L.A. You know I don't even know what you look like."

Marvin felt uncomfortable. "Let's see on that one."

"Come on. When the series is finished you'll be able to take a break." He added, "What keeps you stuck in that hick town? Is it a woman?"

"There's always a woman," Marvin said evasively. "Hey, Ben, can I ask you a blunt question without offending you?"

"Shoot."

"Have you given out my real name or address to anybody?"

"No. Never. Why do you ask?"

"I'm getting some unusual letters mailed directly to me. They've been postmarked locally."

Ben was silent for a minute. "I swear to you that if someone has discovered your true identity or whereabouts, it has not been through this office. Even my own secretary doesn't know who you are or where you live. Are these letters threatening?"

"Not exactly. But they make it clear they know who I am, and that they know what's going on in my life."

"You might want to go to the police."

"No," Marvin said. "Then I'd have no privacy. Is it possible that someone has sneaked a peek at your files?"

"It's out of the question. Besides, if the letters have been mailed locally, the leak has got to be on your end."

"Good point. I apologize for asking."

"No problem," Ben said. "It's probably some crazy teenager who's followed you to your P.O. box. You know how kids can be at that age."

"I do indeed," Marvin said.

They exchanged goodbyes and Marvin glanced at the clock. It was eleven-forty—time to pay Shelly Quade a call.

CHAPTER 5

Shelly greeted him at the door wearing old blue jeans and a thick, frumpy gray sweater. She looked great anyway. It was another one of those cold late-autumn Oregon days and Marvin was chilled from his dash over on his bike. Shelly led him inside to a blazing fire. Her parents were still out of town. He didn't believe, however, that they were going to enjoy a repeat of last night's blissful bubbles. Shelly seemed to be in a serious mood. She curled up on the couch, and he sat on a nearby chair. A pile of official-looking papers sat on the coffee table. Shelly nodded to them.

"Those are for you," she said.

"What are they?"

"The police report on Harry's suicide. The autopsy report is attached."

71

"How did you manage to get ahold of those?"

"Harry's mother requested them a while ago when I told her I believed her son had been murdered."

"Did Harry's mother believe you when you told her?"

Shelly shook her head. "No."

"Have you read the reports?"

"Yes. Closely."

"Is there anything in the reports that leads you to believe he was murdered?" he asked.

She sighed. "Not really. That's why I want you to study them."

"I'm no smarter than you are. I'm certainly no smarter than the police. I want to be blunt right from the beginning, Shelly, so that you don't get any false hopes. I don't think I'm going to be able to help you with this matter."

Shelly looked at him. "How well did you know Harry?"

Well enough to know he was strong competition.

Harry Paster had been a star athlete for Sesa High—both an outstanding receiver on the football team and an excellent guard on the basketball team. Like Triad, a close friend of his, he had been a well-built young man, and handsome. But unlike Triad, Harry had had a brain too. Marvin had shared a chemistry class with him and Harry had done at least as well as he had, if not better. Marvin liked him until Harry tried to steal Shelly away from him. That was a joke—just a line Marvin used to feed himself when he was feeling jealous. Actually, Harry had been going out with Shelly several months before Marvin had managed to stake a claim to her. The fact that Shelly had agreed to go out with him while she was seeing Harry had led Marvin to believe her relationship with Harry couldn't have been that deep. He had changed his mind, of course, when Harry had died and Shelly became so despondent.

Harry had been an unusually quiet young man for a popular athlete. Often Marvin noticed him staring off into the distance during class. Marvin had assumed he was daydreaming about Shelly, but realized after Harry's suicide that his thoughts must have been of a much darker nature.

Yet Marvin was surprised to learn that Harry had taken the big jump.

He had never asked himself if Shelly had had anything to do with Harry taking it.

Until now.

Shelly continued to watch him across the coffee table, waiting for him to answer her question.

"He seemed like a nice guy," Marvin said.

"Did he seem crazy?"

Marvin paused. "No."

"You hesitate. Why?"

Marvin spoke carefully. "He was introspective."

"So what? A lot of people are. You're introspective."

Marvin was curious that she saw him that way. But it wasn't the time to pursue the point. "It's my understanding that people who commit suicide often lapse into long deep silences, especially just before they do away with themselves."

"People in love do that as well," Shelly responded, and there was a note of irritation in her voice.

Marvin took a deep breath. He was not enjoying the conversation. He was beginning to believe Shelly needed professional help to get her over her fixation.

"Was Harry in love with you?" he asked.

Shelly looked at the fire, the orange glow warm on the side of her beautiful face. "I suppose," she said softly.

"Did you do anything to hurt him just before he committed—before he died?"

The question seemed to amuse her, but in a sad way. "I went out with you."

Marvin started to stand. "Shelly—"

"No, wait." She reached out for him. "Please don't leave. I shouldn't have said that. Come, sit beside me. I'm sorry."

He took her hand and let himself be pulled down on the couch beside her. Her fingers were warm and he had to fight an urge to kiss her. And five seconds ago he had been ready to leave.

"I accept your apology," Marvin said. "But what do you want me to do? I don't know how thoroughly the police investigated, but I assume they did a good job."

"That's my point. They didn't. They found Harry floating facedown in the lake, couldn't find a murder weapon or a murder suspect nearby, and closed the book on the case."

Marvin tried a different tack. "You said last night you didn't know who killed him. Do you have any suspects?"

"No."

"Do you have any possible motive?" he asked.

"No."

"So basically you're saying that Harry must have been murdered because you know that he wouldn't have killed himself."

"Yes."

"That doesn't give us a lot to go on."

Shelly reached down and picked up the reports. "That's why I want you to study these." She handed him the papers. "You can talk to Harry's mother if you'd like. Harry's father left them when he was a little kid. He had only one parent. I told her you might be calling."

Marvin wished he'd never gotten involved. "I'll study the reports. That's all I can promise at this point. If I come up with anything I'll let you know."

"When?"

"I don't know when. Maybe never."

"I mean, when am I going to see you again?" She leaned over and kissed him on the cheek. "I want to see you again soon." When he didn't respond right away, she sat back, worried. "What are you thinking?"

"Nothing."

"Tell me."

"I was wondering what really matters to you."

She was cautious. "What do you mean?"

He studied her closely—usually a pleasant pastime. And he didn't see anything he didn't like, and that troubled him even more. Because she was asking him for the ridiculous and he was going to do it simply because she asked. That wasn't the best way to start a relationship.

"Nothing," he said.

"Marvin."

"What?"

She snuggled closer. "I really care about you. And I know that what I'm asking is a little weird. It's just that I can't ask anybody else for help. No one who's got your brains. Do you understand?"

"I suppose," he said.

"You didn't answer my question. When can we go out again?"

He shrugged. "I'm not that busy. Whenever you want."

"How about Monday night?"

"How about tonight?" he asked.

"No good. I'm busy."

"Monday would be fine."

"Want to go to Pella again?" she asked.

He smiled. Maybe he was overreacting to her interest in Harry. He should just enjoy himself— enjoy her. "On my bike?" he asked.

She nodded. "We can stop at the bridge again."

Somehow the reference disturbed him, but he didn't know why. "You won't mind the cold?" he asked.

She let go of him and stared once more into the fire. Her sorrow was never that far away. "No," she said. "I like the cold."

CHAPTER 6

Marvin went to the library after leaving Shelly's house. He couldn't solve his own fictional murder mystery so he figured he might as well try to crack Shelly's. Once at the library he dug through the year-old stacks of Sesa *Bulletins* for articles on Harry's death. He found five. He vaguely remembered reading a couple of them last November. For some reason, even though Harry's suicide had been the talk at school for several weeks, he had avoided involving himself in the subject. Two of the articles were accompanied by the same picture of Harry. Nice haircut, sad expression—the kind of photo that would haunt a mother after her boy was gone.

Had he felt grief at Harry's death? Yes, he could remember being upset when he heard the news. Yet his thoughts had quickly turned to how the suicide would affect Shelly. Now, at least, he knew the answer to that.

Marvin collected his papers, along with the reports Shelly had given him, and made himself comfortable in the reading section of the library. To his surprise he found two girls sitting across from him—they looked like freshmen—reading his books. They appeared thoroughly entranced so he didn't mentally chide them for not buying the books so he could receive more royalties.

Marvin had a small notepad and pen with him, which he always kept in his pocket in case he had a sudden inspiration or interesting idea for a story. He took them out and laid them on the seat beside him. He decided to read through the newspaper articles first—to get an overview. Then he would go over the police and coroner reports. He was a slow reader. Like many authors he read every word.

Two hours later—his reading complete—Marvin had a more thorough understanding of the case of Harry Paster.

Harry had disappeared the night of Friday, November 12. The last person to see him alive was Triad Tyler. According to Triad, they had purchased a couple of six-packs early in the evening, drunk them in Sesa Park by the lake, and parted company close to midnight in front of Harry's house. Triad had dropped Harry off. That was the last time Triad or anyone saw Harry Paster—alive.

Harry's body was found floating facedown in Sesa Lake the following Monday morning, November 15. He was discovered by Sid Green, a senior citizen who often fished before dawn from a rowboat. Sid pulled the body to shore and called the police, who arrived fifteen minutes later. The officer—Maxwell Farmer—reported nothing unusual about the condition of the body. The coroner, in a detailed report, had more to add.

1. Harry had a broken neck and a fractured skull.
2. Harry's palms were blistered.
3. Harry had oil stains on his fingers.
4. Harry had an unusual number of broken blood capillaries in his lower extremities.

It was the coroner's belief that Harry had died by diving headfirst off the cliff into the lake. Although the cliff was not excessively high—one hundred two feet—the water at the base of the cliff was only fifteen feet deep. It was the coroner's opinion that Harry had struck his head on the soft mud bottom and died instantly. The injuries to his neck and skull formed the basis of this opinion. There were no obvious signs of struggle on the body. Harry had almost certainly not been attacked. The blistered palms and broken blood capillaries, although unusual, were not considered significant. Harry could have got oil on his hands performing any number of tasks before committing suicide.

The coroner, however, did not even attempt to address the broken capillaries.

The coroner put the time of Harry's death at approximately 12:00 A.M. Monday morning, six hours before his body was found. But the coroner admitted it was possible Harry had died as much as six hours earlier. Cold water greatly slowed down the process a body went through in the hours following death. Harry had not even begun to show signs of rigor mortis when he was pulled from the lake.

As they say, those were the facts.

Unlike Shelly, Marvin found much in the material to make him smell something fishy. To assume someone jumped off a cliff simply because no one had seen him pushed seemed quite a leap in deductive reasoning. But he could understand the thinking of the police and the coroner. They were offering the simplest explanation, and in lieu of evidence substantiating a different conclusion, they were going to stick with it. Marvin could also see that it would be next to impossible to prove that Harry was pushed, no matter what research he did. If a witness hadn't come forward yet, he or she was not going to come forward. It was a shame in a way—the most likely alternative scenario was practically closed to him before he could begin. Yet he was more open to the idea of murder than before. He had been wrong to tell Shelly that since the police had closed the book on the case it should remain closed.

Maybe Harry hadn't jumped or been pushed. Perhaps there was a third alternative.

Marvin was frankly surprised Shelly hadn't informed him of these other mysterious odds and ends. Of course, she wasn't the amateur sleuth he was.

The oil stains on Harry's palms could have come from anywhere; that was true. At this point it would be fruitless to speculate on them. Later, though, they might be important.

The broken blood capillaries in Harry's legs were also difficult to fathom. Marvin hadn't a clue what could have caused them. He would have to do more research.

The blistered palms, on the other hand, were intriguing from the start. Both the coroner and the police said there were no signs of struggle on the body. It seemed to Marvin a narrow perception on their part of what constituted struggle. If a man was thrown into a dry well and held prisoner, and he tried to climb out, he would probably get blisters. The blisters would be a sign of struggle in response to an *indirect* physical attack.

Was it possible Harry had been kept captive somewhere before he was killed? The missing time, between when Harry disappeared and when his body was found, was intriguing. Marvin could not believe he had been unaware of that fact at the time of Harry's death, yet he had absolutely no memory of it.

Marvin jotted down the two dates—Friday, November 12, the day Harry had disappeared, and Monday, November 15, the day Harry had died. Where had Harry been on that intervening Saturday and Sunday? Marvin thought, and it took him several minutes to remember where *he* had been on any of those days.

Finally he remembered. He, Marvin, had been out with Shelly the day Harry had disappeared. And there was one other small point.

November twelfth—that's Shelly's birthday for godsakes!

How could he have forgotten such a crucial event on such a critical day? It boggled Marvin's mind. If he were a psychiatrist he would have said he had subconsciously blocked the information. But he wasn't a psychiatrist. He was a mystery writer. He returned to the facts. If there was a murderer he needed suspects.

He had gone out with Shelly Friday night to celebrate her birthday. Curiously enough they had done almost exactly what they had done the day before. They had ridden to Pella on his bike, eaten dinner, seen a movie, and driven home. The only difference was that they had not stopped on the bridge, nor had they climbed into the hot tub together. Where was Harry that night? The newspapers and the police report said he was out with Triad, drinking beer. In any murder situation the last person to see the victim alive was immediately a suspect. But Marvin's memory—now that it had got a jump start—was suddenly coming up with all kinds of interesting little details.

Triad could not be a suspect because Harry had died sometime between six Sunday evening and twelve midnight. And during that time Triad had been in a medium-size town fifty miles east of Sesa named Canteen. The football team had been in the play-offs and the game had been postponed from Saturday night to Sunday night because of poor weather. Not that the delay had helped much. It had poured throughout Sunday's game, and then afterward, after Sesa had been soundly defeated, the Sesa coaches decided that because of the rain it would be better to bus the players home on Monday morning. Marvin had not gone to the game, but had heard about the particulars at school on Monday. When Harry's body had been discovered in the lake, his absence from the game had naturally been discussed. Of course, if a guy was about to kill himself he didn't usually go play football beforehand. Marvin decided to check on whether Triad had spent Sunday night with his football buddies, but he was already confident that Triad could not have killed Harry.

If Harry had been killed, which—a few curious details aside—he probably hadn't been. But for the sake of his investigation Marvin had to assume temporarily that there had been a crime. Why else would he continue it?

He needed more suspects. Who had hated Harry? Harry had been a loner. The only people close to him had been Shelly and Triad. And Shelly wouldn't have killed Harry and Triad couldn't have.

The only person Marvin could think of who had any motivation at all to murder Harry was he, Marvin. For the love of Shelly Quade. That was a great reason. Waste the competition. Marvin chuckled aloud at the thought. He would have remembered something like that.

Marvin got up and went to the pay phone at the front of the library. He checked the white pages and found Sid Green's address—the elderly gentleman who had discovered Harry's body. He considered calling but decided to drop by. He was pretty certain old Sid would have nothing valuable to tell him.

Sid Green was sitting on his front porch reading a newspaper when Marvin arrived. He had to be in his seventies, going by the number of wrinkles on his face, but he wasn't decrepit. Marvin was reminded that here was a man who went fishing before dawn, and if the police report could be believed, had single-handedly dragged Harry's body from the lake.

"What can I do for you, young fellow?" Mr. Green asked, setting aside his paper. He had a huge package of red licorice resting in his lap and what appeared to be a good wad of it in his mouth. He chewed his licorice slowly, with the satisfaction of a six-year-old boy. It was a cold day to be sitting outside and reading, but Mr. Green was bundled up in a fat wool sweater that Mrs. Green had probably knitted for him when they were courting. Marvin came up the steps and offered his hand.

"My name's Marvin," Marvin said, shaking the gentleman's hand. "I was a friend of Harry Paster. Do you remember him?"

Mr. Green reached for another red licorice stick. "I haven't found that many dead bodies in my days while I've been fishing. I remember him. Never saw such blue cheeks in my life." He took a bite of his candy. "I'm sorry, young fellow. I shouldn't have spoken of him that way. You said he was your friend?"

"Yes, but I'm over it. The grief, I mean." Marvin glanced up and down the street and wondered what the hell he was doing on a Saturday afternoon quizzing a seventy-year-old man. He continued, "But I still have some questions about the way Harry died. I was wondering if I could ask you about what you saw that morning."

"I saw a young boy floating facedown in the water. Hell, I don't know what else to say. He was dead as a firefly in a snowstorm."

"Did you actually pull him out of the water?"

Mr. Green nodded with pride. "That I did. Hooked my line onto the collar of his leather jacket and rowed us both to shore. Got my wind up doing it, but I couldn't leave the lad floating out there." Mr. Green sighed and shook his head and had another bite of licorice. "They say he jumped. What a pity. When I was that age the only thing I thought about was girls and sex. I'd spend all day thinking about them. Not that I ever had sex. I don't know what's wrong with young folk nowadays. They can have all the sex they want and they still ain't happy. Makes no sense to me."

"It makes no sense to me either," Marvin said. "I've read the police and coroner reports on the case. They say there were no obvious marks of struggle on the body. Do you remember any?"

Mr. Green thought for a long moment. "Can't say I do."

"Do you remember the blisters on Harry's palms?"

"Why did he have blisters?"

"I don't know."

"I don't remember no blisters."

"They were there. You probably just missed them." Marvin was already losing enthusiasm for the interrogation. "What was Harry wearing when you found him?"

Mr. Green had to think again. "Like I said, he had on a brown leather jacket and I think a sweater underneath. The jacket was puffed up if you know what I mean. I don't know what kind of pants he was wearing."

"Were there any stains on his clothes?" Marvin asked.

"What kind of stains?"

"Any kind. Food stains. Bloodstains."

"I didn't say he was bleeding."

"I understand that. I was just asking about the condition of his clothes. Look, I should leave you in peace. I'll go. If you can think of anything you can call me at—"

"There were some marks on his jacket," Mr. Green interrupted.

Marvin paused. "What kind of marks?"

Mr. Green gestured to his armpits. "They were like burns on the leather."

"The leather had been burned?"

"No. Not actually burned. It was more like the leather had been rubbed raw."

"By what?" Marvin asked.

"I don't know."

"Could you give me more details about the marks? Did they wrap around the chest under the armpits?"

"Yes."

"How thick were they?"

"Narrow."

"Narrow?" Marvin repeated.

"Yeah."

"Were the marks on the back of his jacket as well?"

"I think so."

"You're not sure?"

"No. Maybe. Yeah, I think there were marks there as well."

Marvin considered. "Mr. Green, could those marks have been made by a rope?"

"I don't know of any rope that would burn leather like that."

If the rope was scraped across the leather again and again it might.

Marvin moved to leave. "Thank you, Mr. Green. You've been most helpful."

CHAPTER 7

Marvin went to the Paster residence next. He called Harry's mother ahead of time. He wasn't sure exactly what Shelly had told the woman and didn't want to do anything that might add to her grief. But Mrs. Paster said she'd be happy to see him.

She was a good-looking woman, which was not surprising given her son's striking looks. She was also relatively young to have had an eighteen-year-old son; she must have had Harry in her late teens. She let Marvin in and offered him a cup of coffee and a plate of freshly baked chocolate-chip cookies, which he accepted gratefully. They sat at the kitchen table together, an old hand-carved wooden clock ticking above their heads.

"Shelly says you two are good friends," Mrs.

Paster remarked as she brought the coffeepot to the table. "Cream or sugar?"

"Both, thank you. Yes, that's true. I've known Shelly since—high school. I mean, since the beginning of school." He added, "I knew Harry as well. He was in my chemistry class."

She smiled quickly, and it was sad to see the pain still at the edges of her smile. "Harry always liked chemistry."

Marvin tried one of the cookies. "He was an excellent student."

She spoke with too much pleasure. "Wasn't he, though? He would read those textbooks like they were Mack Slate thrillers."

Marvin almost gagged on the cookie. "God."

"Are you all right, Marvin?"

He cleared his throat and reached for his coffee. "Yes, I just get choked-up sometimes when I— choke on my food." He took a sip of the steaming beverage. The woman made excellent coffee and Marvin was something of a connoisseur when it came to the stuff. He drank gallons of coffee when he was writing at full speed. "You must be wondering why I wanted to see you."

Mrs. Paster's hand shook as she raised her own cup to her lips. "Shelly said you were checking into where Harry was the Saturday and Sunday before he was found."

That was part of what he was doing at Mrs. Paster's house. But he hadn't told Shelly that. Shelly had obviously read the material as closely as he had and was anticipating his moves. Yet she was vague when he had questioned her about the reports. He found that curious.

"I'm trying to learn where he was, yes," Marvin said. "Do you have any ideas?"

"I'm afraid not."

"Triad says he dropped Harry back here close to midnight. Did you hear Harry come in?"

"No. But Harry was fond of staying out late on the weekends." She shrugged; it was more of a tremble than a casual gesture. "He was a grown boy. I often went to sleep before he came home."

"Do you believe Triad when he says he brought Harry back here?"

Mrs. Paster blinked. "Of course. Those two were the best of friends. They'd known each other since they were toddlers. Triad wouldn't have lied about something like that."

"I'm sure he wouldn't have. Do you have the jacket Harry was wearing when he died?"

"Pardon?"

"Harry's leather jacket. Do you have it here in the house?"

"Yes."

"Could I see it, please?" Marvin asked.

Mrs. Paster stood unsteadily. "I think it's in the garage. Could you give me a minute?"

"Sure."

Harry drank his coffee and ate his cookies while Mrs. Paster was gone. He felt guilty for even being in the house. He believed it was because he was in love with the girlfriend of the woman's dead son. In fact, if he was totally honest with himself, one of the main reasons he was conducting his investigation was to keep Shelly happy so that she would sit naked in the Jacuzzi with him again. There was a picture of Harry on the wall in the kitchen. It stared at him with accusing eyes.

"Here it is," Mrs. Paster said as she reentered the room with a badly stained brown leather jacket in her arms. She handed it to him quickly, glad to be rid of it. The water had done a number on the jacket. The leather felt like parchment under Marvin's probing fingers.

The marks were as the old man had described and Marvin had pictured. They circled around the chest, under the armpits to the back. It was true they could have been caused by a rope scraping against the leather, yet, now that he had the jacket in hand, Marvin couldn't imagine how Harry could have been successfully tied up for two days and made the marks fighting against his binds. There were no rope burns around the waist, or anywhere except for the single line of marks on the upper portion of the jacket. Surely a murderer would have more thoroughly tied Harry up if he'd wanted to keep him in one place.

Yet Harry had had those blisters. Rope could give a guy blisters.

"Did he have a sweater on under this when he was found?" Marvin asked.

"Yes," Mrs. Paster said. "Why do you ask?"

"The jacket would have been enough to keep him warm during the daytime, but at night he'd have needed a sweater to be comfortable." What he was also thinking was that the coroner had made no mention of rope burns on Harry's skin, which could have been the case even if Harry had been tied up for a couple of days—as long as he'd been wearing enough layers under the jacket to protect his skin from the rope. Marvin added, "What was Harry wearing when he went out with Triad Friday night?"

"I don't know. I didn't see him go out. I'd gone to dinner with a friend. But Harry often wore this jacket. It was his favorite."

"Did it have these marks on it before he died?" Marvin asked.

"No."

"Did the police or the coroner say anything to you about how they might have been caused?" Marvin asked.

"No."

"Did you ask them?"

"Yes. They said they weren't important." Mrs. Paster paused. "Do you think they're important?"

"Maybe." He set the jacket aside. "Would you mind if I kept the jacket for a few days?"

Mrs. Paster hesitated. "That would be fine. But please bring it back when you're done."

"I will. I promise."

Mrs. Paster looked uncomfortable. "Forgive me for asking, but why are you checking into the details surrounding my son's death?"

"Shelly asked me to. She must have told you. She believes Harry was murdered."

Mrs. Paster stirred her coffee. "She mentioned that to me."

"Mrs. Paster, can I ask you a delicate question?"

She looked up. "You want to know if I think my son committed suicide?"

"I'm sorry," Marvin muttered, embarrassed at the position he had placed them both in. Mrs. Paster glanced at the picture of Harry on the wall. But now the boy's eyes weren't so accusing.

"I don't think any mother can believe her son would take his own life," Mrs. Paster said softly. "Harry died a year ago and I wonder if I believe it yet." A shudder went across her features. "But if you're asking me if Harry was unhappy I would have to say yes."

"Do you know what he was unhappy about?" Marvin asked. He remembered Shelly's comment to him on the couch. *"I went out with you."* But surely that wouldn't have been reason enough to push Harry over the edge, not unless the guy had had deep psychological problems.

"No," Mrs. Paster said. "I asked Shelly but—"

"Yes."

Mrs. Paster made a small despairing gesture with her hand. "She didn't know."

"I see."

"Do you know her well?" Mrs. Paster asked suddenly, and there was an edge to the question. The woman wanted to know if he had taken Harry's place in Shelly's life.

"We're just friends," Marvin said tactfully. "I'm sorry I didn't answer your question of a moment ago—why Shelly wanted me to dig into your son's death. I honestly don't know the answer to that. Except that I knew Harry, and liked him, and I'm good at figuring things out. I guess those are the reasons Shelly asked me."

Mrs. Paster nodded sadly. "The police say it was suicide. I wish I didn't believe them."

"Sometimes it's hard to know what to believe," Marvin agreed, and his own words made him wonder.

CHAPTER 8

When Marvin got home his mother was watching *Casablanca,* a movie she had seen two hundred times. Her eyes hardly stirred from the screen as he walked across the living room in front of her. It was five o'clock and getting dark. The sun never set without her being drunk and she was drunk now.

"Hi, Mom," he said. He leaned over and kissed her cheek. "Have a nice day?"

"It was all right." She lifted a lethargic hand and touched his side. "Be a dear, Marvin, and make me some popcorn."

"Why don't I cook you some real food? We have chicken in the icebox. I could grill it and put on some potatoes."

"Popcorn would be fine. Is there butter?"

Marvin sighed. "There's butter."

In the kitchen he found Ann cooking them both dinner. Ann had given up trying to get their mom to eat anything substantial. Their mom subsisted on popcorn, See's Candies, white toast, and fast-food pizza and tacos. And, of course, booze.

Ann was a good cook for a kid. She had taken the chicken and sautéed it in lemon and garlic sauce, and sprinkled it with bits of saffron. She was a master when it came to stuffed potatoes and the one waiting for him was fat with sour cream, butter, and some kind of cheese from Switzerland. Marvin let Ann put the final touches on their meal while he got his mother's popcorn ready. But when he returned to the living room with the stuff, his mom was passed out on the couch. He set the bowl beside her and kissed her once more on the cheek. He worried that one day he was going to find her in a similar position, curled up on the sofa, but dead.

He and Ann ate in the kitchen. Ann wanted to know what he had been doing all day. She was worried about his book—everyone was. He told her there was nothing to worry about.

"Because there's no book," he added.

"Are you getting any ideas?" Ann asked.

"I am. One."

"What is it?"

Marvin didn't pause. The words jumped out of his mouth. God knew where they came from. "I don't believe Ann McGaffer was killed in the lake," he said. "I don't even think she was killed near the lake."

"How did she get there then?"

This time Marvin did pause to think, and what he'd been about to say slipped away and he couldn't get it back. "I'm not sure," he muttered.

"I hope you get more ideas soon. I don't want to end up out on the streets."

"I hear they can be hard on little girls," Marvin agreed.

Ann shook a layer of pepper onto her potato. "Did you see Shelly today?"

"Yes."

"What did you do?"

Marvin shrugged. "Nothing."

"Did you kiss her?"

"That's none of your business."

Ann nodded. "You kissed her."

"Actually, I didn't. We mainly talked about Harry Paster. Shelly thinks he was murdered. She wants me to find the guy and bring him to justice."

"Are you kidding me?"

"I'm very serious," Marvin said.

Ann's reaction surprised him. She looked scared. "I bet she wants something else. Remember what the letter said. She doesn't love you like you think she does."

Marvin was annoyed. "How the hell would a complete stranger know how Shelly feels about me?"

Ann shook her head. "You never know."

They finished their dinner and Ann stayed in the kitchen to do the dishes and clean up. Marvin went up to his room to write a complete novel in a few hours. Staring at the blank screen didn't do anything to soothe his nerves. Finally he picked up the phone and called Shelly. She had said Sunday night was no good but he hadn't asked about tonight. He was missing her in a bad way. He couldn't understand the hold she had over him, but he understood that nobody in love ever did. She answered promptly. She sounded out of breath.

"Hello?"

"Hi. This is Marvin. How are you doing?"

"Good," she said. "Did you find out anything?"

"A few things. I'd like to talk to you about them. Can I come over?"

"When?"

"Tonight sometime."

"I told you, tonight's no good."

He paused. "Why not?"

"I'm busy."

He felt a stab of rejection and was mad at himself. He was acting as if he owned the girl just because she had sat naked in a Jacuzzi with him. "All right. I guess I'll have to wait until Monday night. We're still going out, aren't we?"

"Sure," she said. "But tell me what you found out."

"Nothing definite. But I am now open to the possibility that Harry was murdered."

She didn't seem surprised. "You just keep working on it. I know you're the one who'll clear Harry's name."

"Maybe." He strained his ears. He thought he heard water running in the background. "I'm looking forward to Monday night."

A note of flirting entered her voice. "So am I. I

think it will be divine." Abruptly her tone changed to brisk and businesslike. "I've got to go now."

"'Bye, Shelly." Marvin set down the phone. She was unpredictable, that girl was. He wondered if she was going out on a date then, and with whom.

Marvin lay down on his bed. He'd take a nap and when he woke up he'd start writing. He decided it didn't matter which direction he went in—he'd just follow his instincts.

He was asleep in a minute.

He was dreaming in two.

He was a character in his *The Mystery of Silver Lake* series. Only he wasn't the same character in each scene. He kept changing into different people, and like an omniscient god, he knew what all his characters were feeling and thinking—when he was in their heads.

In the beginning he was Ann McGaffer—sweet Ann, who loved the unfaithful and volatile Clyde Fountain, and who was also fond of the dear and sympathetic Mike Madison, a spiritual brother. Marvin followed Ann as she went to school during the first days of the story. He had to follow her because he was inside her body. She was so beautiful. Everywhere she went heads turned. But not all the people behind these heads were happy to see her. Many were jealous, and Ann felt the hate flowing from their sidelong glances. The price of popularity—and no one was more popular than Ann.

Except she didn't know how much she had going for her.

She was so unhappy.

She meets Clyde at lunch and asks where he was the previous night. She had called so many times. He just gets angry and won't say. How can he? Marvin shifts to inside Clyde's head and sees that Clyde had been with Jessica Moss the previous night. Jessica—Ann's best friend, the only person in the whole world she trusts completely. Clyde had not only been with Jessica—he had been making passionate love to her on the hood of her green Alfa Romeo.

Clyde and Ann have a short but intense fight and Ann stalks off—Marvin was now back in her brain. She runs into the sweet and smiling Mike Madison. Mike listens patiently while Ann explains how hard it is being with Clyde. Then Mike takes her back to his place and somehow manages to get her clothes off. They make love in front of his fireplace. The sex is great for both of them, but afterward Mike feels guilty because Ann is involved with another guy and Ann feels guilty because to do so is her natural state. Yet it's possible Mike's guilt is only an act—Marvin can't exactly get into his head, which is strange because Mike is the most like him. Mike and Ann agree they must never have sex again, at least not in the immediate future. But they do it again ten minutes after making this vow, and it's better than the first time.

Meanwhile Marvin experiences a leap in consciousness and finds Clyde out drinking with his best friend, Terry Rogers. Clyde is telling Terry what a bitch Ann has become and Terry encourages Clyde to dump Ann while the dumping is good. But

Marvin can see that Terry is only telling Clyde this because he wants Ann for himself.

In Silver Lake everyone is screwing everyone else.

But time goes on. Days and pages pass. Marvin feels the tension building in everyone. Clyde hates Ann but still lusts after her. Mike loves Ann and hates Clyde. Terry thinks he loves Ann but really hates her, along with Clyde and Mike. But life is hardest for Ann. Her father, Bill McGaffer, comes in late one night, drunk, and abuses her, making her want to commit suicide. Then her crazy younger brother, Harold McGaffer, who thinks the Antichrist is reincarnated in the holes of doughnuts throughout the western United States, tries to convince Ann that Clyde is trying to kill her, leading her to believe she is a tragic victim in a poorly written soap opera. Ann often feels like this anyway.

Then all goes dark and cold. Marvin can feel an icy spray beating against Ann's soaked flesh. As in the beginning, so it is in the end. He is inside Ann and there is terrible pain. He sees a flash of white light, a scene glimpsed in the high beams of a distant automobile. He steps out of her ravaged body and turns a hundred eighty degrees in space and sees behind him. The horror of the moment shakes him to the core. Poor Ann—she is hanging by a rope tied round her waist in the middle of the night, dangling off a bridge in a cruel breeze. She is screaming, she is dying, but no one can hear her, and in the end, she realizes, no one cares.

Except Marvin, who always loved her.

Even when he knew she was as corrupt as the rest.

Marvin woke to a small hand shaking him. "What?" he asked, bolting upright with a start, his heart pounding. Ann was sitting on the bed beside him, her face twisted with anxiety.

"Marvin," she croaked.

"What is it?" he demanded, coming fully alert. There was some noise coming from downstairs but he wasn't sure what it was.

Ann wept. "Daddy's here. He's breaking things."

Marvin leapt off his bed and ran downstairs, Ann following. For such a menacing bully, his father was not a big man. Only five eight and not more than a hundred forty pounds. Yet what muscles were there, were difficult to subdue when he was enraged. Marvin had only fought with his father twice, and he couldn't have said either of them had come away victorious either time. His mom was standing in front of the TV screaming at his dad. She may have been protecting the picture tube. Marvin's dad had a lamp in his shaking hands and it looked as if he wanted to ram it through Humphrey Bogart's face. They were both exhaling eighty proof—it was amazing that someone's breath hadn't caught fire yet.

"You are a sick woman and I am going to cure you!" his father screamed. "Now get out of my way!"

"Marvin, stop him!" his mother cried.

His father whirled on him. "What are you doing here?"

"I live here," Marvin said calmly. "Put that thing down. It's our best lamp."

"I don't give a damn about your best anything!" his dad yelled. "I am sick and tired of this pathetic family. Every time I come over here the TV is on. Well, I'm turning it off for good."

With that pronouncement, his dad reached out, grabbed his mother by the hair and threw her onto the floor. Ann ran to her aid. Before Marvin could stop him, his dad had rammed the top of the lamp into the picture tube, which had cost Marvin five hundred dollars last month to replace. The thing imploded like a miniature bomb. Glass sprayed the entire living room, particularly Ann, who stood sheltering her mother. So light and fragile, Ann was almost knocked down by the shock wave. Dazed, she tried to pull the shards from her hair and ended up cutting herself. Blood covered her hands and she stared at them with a blank expression.

Now that made Marvin mad.

Marvin charged his dad, without a clear plan as to what he was doing. They collided in front of the TV and went down on the glass-covered carpet. They rolled on top of each other, scrambling for an advantage. Marvin had the advantage this time. He was younger and stronger and he was not drunk. Alcohol brought on his dad's rage, and gave him strength, but the guy had drunk one too many. Marvin was surprised at how easily he was able to pin his father beneath his knees.

"Stop it, Dad!" he shouted at him.

"Bastard son!" his dad yelled back. He spit in Marvin's face.

Something happened to Marvin right then. It wasn't so much the spit, or the broken tube, or even Ann's bloody hands. It was everything combined, perhaps, and maybe something else he didn't understand.

Marvin lost it. He yanked his dad to his feet and punched the guy in the face with everything he had. His father crumpled to the floor, his face bloody, and Marvin yanked him to his feet again and kicked him hard in the groin. His dad was screaming for mercy when Marvin yanked him to his feet for the third time. But there was no mercy in Marvin. He pulled back his fist again.

"Marvin!" his mother cried, grabbing hold of his arm. Marvin looked over at her and didn't see her for a moment. He saw an older version of Ann McGaffer instead. An aged Ann brought back to life for the moment to prevent him from fulfilling his destiny. Because right then there was nothing more satisfying in all the world to Marvin than the thought of beating his father's face to an unrecognizable purple pulp.

"Marvin," Ann said, and he had to look down to find her. She was tugging on his shirt, staining it with the blood that had begun to trickle over her arms. He was frightened by her fear, because it was not directed at her father, but at him. "Let him go," Ann whimpered.

Marvin released his father. The man fell to the floor in a lump of pain. His mother and Ann knelt to attend to him. Marvin turned and fled upstairs to his room. There he grabbed his helmet, wallet, checkbook, and Harry's leather jacket. He didn't even look into the living room as he ran down the stairs and out of the house. He climbed on his bike and roared off into the night. He drove as though he were fleeing the scene of a murder he had committed.

CHAPTER 9

The night air was a healing balm for Marvin's anger. After racing for half an hour on the open road, he began to come to his senses. He cut his speed from ninety miles an hour to fifty. He had to look around to figure out where he was. He had left town on Highway 16, he recalled—he must be forty miles east of Sesa now. Here the land received far less rain and consequently was more desolate. He slowly turned his bike around and headed back toward town. But he had no intention of going straight home. He was frightened, but not of his dad. He wondered if his mother and sister hadn't been there would he have killed his father? His hand still ached from the punch he had thrown. It was possible he had broken a finger or two. That would sure speed up the typing of his manuscript.

Yet he was not ready to accept the blame for what had happened. His dad belonged in a zoo. One thing for sure—that guy was never coming to their house again. Marvin swore he'd go to the police to get a restraining order.

I'll buy a gun if I have to.

A silly thought. What would he do with a gun?

Marvin entered Sesa forty-five minutes later. Highway 16 ran right in front of the post office and on impulse Marvin swung into the lot and parked his bike. It was blind impulse, he thought, as he walked to the door with the broken lock that no one bothered to have fixed. He had already checked his mail, and there couldn't have been another delivery that day. Of course, the last letter he had received from his mysterious adviser had not come through the usual channels. Marvin wanted to see if another note had been stuffed inside his box.

There was one. He tore it open and held it toward the streetlight just outside the building.

THEY ARE PLOTTING TO KILL YOU
AS YOU READ THIS.

"Who are they?" Marvin asked the empty room. Once more he glanced around to see if he was being observed. And he had the feeling that a pair of eyes, maybe two, were watching him crumple up the note and throw it in the wastebasket. There were a few cars parked up and down the road. There could be people sitting in them, in the dark, and he'd never know.

What was he going to do now? Go to the police?

He'd have to tell them he was Mack Slate. Then his dad would know about his millions, and his millions of fans would know about him—that he was not so handsome, not so glamorous, only a kid. He wondered if his fans' finding out wasn't the real reason he kept his identity secret. It was much easier to become a legend when people didn't know how human you were.

Was the person who was sending the notes accurate? He had asked himself the same question this morning. What had the person said so far? He knew who he was. Shelly did not love him as he thought. And somebody—*they*—were plotting to kill him. Obviously the person was right on the first point. He couldn't be stuffing Mack Slate's box every few hours unless he knew that much. What about the second note? Shelly had smoothly put him off about tonight. Was it because she was interested in someone else? Triad for example? Could she have just jumped into the Jacuzzi with good old Marvin because she wanted him chasing after Harry's ghost when he should be . . .

Getting ready to defend himself?

That was absurd. Shelly wasn't plotting to kill him. Nobody wanted him dead, with the possible exception of his dad.

Still, it wouldn't hurt to swing by her place.

Just for a quick look.

Marvin got on his bike and drove toward Shelly's house. He cut the engine when he reached her block and coasted the remainder of the way. That was the trouble with a motorcycle—it was hard to sneak up on anybody. He parked a couple of houses down from hers and left his helmet resting on his seat. He didn't expect to be long.

He could see that her lights were on.

He could hear music as he walked up the steps.

Loud rock 'n' roll music. Party time.

He knocked and waited.

"Shelly?" he called.

But not too loud. Nor did he ring the doorbell. He didn't know what he was thinking, but it must have not been about trust and loyalty because he cracked her front door open a couple of inches and peered inside before calling her name again. He wasn't trying to sneak up on her, he convinced himself; rather, he wanted to surprise her.

Doing what?

Marvin stepped inside. It was warm or he was cold—or both. The music was coming from the living room—Mick Jagger trying to start up a young babe. There was no one in the living room. Yet there were voices, running water. The porch, the Jacuzzi—oh, God. Marvin walked toward it on tiptoe. He knew what he would find. But he had to *know*, which was different. He had to see, which was entirely different.

He crept to the doorway that led out to the porch and peeked around the doorframe.

Then he pulled back and felt warm tears trickle over his freezing cheeks. He kept his sobs choked deep inside.

Shelly was in the Jacuzzi with Triad. There were too many bubbles to be sure but it was a safe bet they were naked. They were definitely kissing and Shelly was moaning. Friday night Marvin. The high point of his young life. Saturday night Triad. Probably just another roll in the hay—or the jets—for the stupid jock. My, wasn't Shelly's schedule crowded. Who would it be Sunday night? Their speech teacher—Mr. Ramar. He was married but that shouldn't bother a girl like Shelly.

"Christ," Marvin whispered, sucking in a burning breath. His lungs felt as if they were on fire. All at once he wanted to do so many crazy things. He wanted to burst in on them and beat the crap out of Triad. But that wouldn't work. Triad was not drunk or out of shape. He would beat the crap out of him. He wanted to call Shelly a two-bit whore. Triad would probably still beat the crap out of him. Finally, he wanted Shelly. Yes, crazy as it sounded, he wished more than anything that it were he who was caressing her in the warm, bubbly water. That she was moaning into his mouth. It was sick—he hated her, but he still wanted her. The whole world was sick.

What he ended up doing was nothing—for the moment. He just stood there behind the wall, trying to breathe in air that tasted of lavender heaven. She must have a whole closet filled with the junk. He honestly thought for a few minutes that he was going to have a heart attack. It didn't help his irregular beat to be listening to their pleasure. He tried to block it out, but then the moans stopped, and they began to talk, and he wanted to listen.

"This is good," Shelly said.

"It doesn't get much better," Triad agreed.

"How long has it been?" she asked.

"Two days."

"Two days too long."

"Where were you last night?" Triad asked.

"Out with Marvin."

Triad chuckled. "That worm? Why?"

"For fun and profit."

"Huh?"

Soft splashes. It sounded as if Shelly was rearranging herself in the tub so that she could be of more service to her man. Marvin simply would not let himself look.

"Do you like that?" she asked in a sly voice.

"Hmmm. I'd like it more if I knew I was the only one you did it to."

Shelly gave a short laugh. "God. You think I had sex with Marvin? Gimme a break. I just went out with him to get him to do a few things for me."

"Like what?" Triad asked.

"None of your business," Shelly said.

Triad was silent for a moment. He may have been enjoying something Marvin had never had a chance to enjoy, and now never would. Tears continued to spill down his face. The worst thing was that he knew even as he shed them that they were only the beginning. He was never going to forget this night.

He was never going to forgive her.

"Are you going out with him again?" Triad asked.

"If it's necessary."

"I don't know if I like this."

"I thought you said you loved it," she said.

"I mean Marvin."

"Why don't you buy his bike? I love riding on it."

"How can I buy something he won't sell? I'll buy another bike."

"No, his is special," she said. "I want his."

"What about what I want? I don't like you going out with him. I won't put up with it."

Shelly sounded amused, not the least bit intimidated. "I'm supposed to see him Monday night."

"Cancel it," Triad said flatly.

Shelly gave it a moment of thought. That was all the bitch needed. "All right. I'll tell him I'm busy. Busy with you."

"What do you want to do Monday night?"

"Screw," she said.

Marvin left the house. When he was outside, standing beside his bike, he thought he was going to throw up. He bowed his head and gagged but nothing came out. His pain was not just emotional, it was physical. There was a cramp in his chest—it was as if his blood had suddenly clotted into a dozen black globs and plugged up his healthy pink arteries. He simply could not catch his breath, and his tears would not stop. *His* girl, *his* Shelly, screwing that poor excuse of a piece of meat. He just couldn't bear the thought of what he had just heard, and it was all he could think about. God had messed up bad when he had designed the human mind. He had forgotten to install an off switch. Marvin wished he could just turn off his brain and pretend the last ten minutes hadn't happened.

But it was happening even as he stood out in the cold by himself. The world was so unfair. He was a good person. He worked hard. He took care of his mother and his sister. He didn't ask for much in return. He just wanted a girl to love, a girl to love him. And here he had to fall for the worst kind of slut. And he was still in love with her! That was why it hurt so much.

Marvin picked up his helmet and climbed on his bike. He couldn't go home. His father might still be there. He didn't want to see anybody anyway. He just wanted to drive and drive until he came to the edge of the world. He started the engine on his bike. He flipped up the plastic visor on his helmet. He would let the wind dry his tears.

A half hour later found him sitting on the bridge that stretched across the Pella River, in the exact spot where he had sat with Shelly. He knew it was the same spot because he remembered the piece of rope he'd plopped down onto that night. That night—God it was only yesterday. A lot could change in twenty-four hours. The sun could blow up and burn all the planets in the solar system to ash in twenty-four hours. He wished the sun would give it serious consideration when it came up the next day.

He was on the bridge for understanding. For revenge.

He believed he could have one if he could find the other.

Marvin picked up the ragged piece of rope and wondered why it was that he had spent half the day chasing a length of rope and its effect on a certain leather jacket while investigating Harry's death, and also why it was that Shelly had carefully maneuvered him to a place where he would sit on just such a piece of rope. Marvin did not believe in coincidences, even when he was plotting his books. That was one of the reasons he couldn't choose just anybody to be Ann's murderer. Because he would have to invent one or two coincidences to substantiate their actions, which he hated to do. He was sure Shelly hated coincidences as much since she was such a fan of his work.

There was no question in his mind that she had wanted to impress upon him the relationship between what was right in front of him and what was missing. The weathered piece of rope he had in his hand was tied to the edge of the bridge and it could have lain out in the cold and wet for a whole year. It had oil stains deeply imbedded in its fibers.

Oil like that on Harry's blistered hands.

Maybe Harry had been hanging on to a rope—this rope—before he died.

Hanging on for life? Or just hanging until he died?

That was an interesting difference, Marvin thought.

He didn't know what the hell Shelly was up to. Did she know how Harry had died? Had she killed him? Did she know who had killed him? Did she want him to know? Or had Harry really committed suicide, and was she trying to drive him to do the same? She was doing a hell of a job at the latter, Marvin thought. The idea of jumping into the icy torrent and washing away into oblivion had never seemed so appealing.

But Harry had probably not jumped, at least not off the cliff into Lake Sesa. Marvin believed he had established that much. There were two old tricks in mystery writing. Lead the reader to believe that the crime had occurred in a place other than *where* it had really happened. And lead the reader into a false sense of *when* the crime had occurred. If he concentrated on the first point, and moved Harry's death from the lake to the bridge, it gave a whole new slant to the matter. Marvin felt justified in doing this. After all, once Harry was dead it would have been no problem for his body to wash down the river and into the lake.

But Marvin was still confused. He knew he had to back up and figure out a scenario that could explain everything he had discovered. The idea that Harry had somehow been hanging from the bridge appeared to be the key, but the bridge was only the beginning. Marvin mentally reviewed the physical evidence.

Point one: the blisters on Harry's palms. They fit in perfectly with the hanging scenario. Harry could have got them trying to pull himself back up onto the bridge.

Point two: the ruptured blood capillaries in Harry's legs. Again, they fit in with the hanging idea. The blood would have pooled into Harry's lower extremities. Had he hung long enough before falling into the water quite a number of small vessels—so Marvin imagined—would have burst.

Point three: the burn marks on Harry's jacket. This was a more complicated piece of evidence than it first appeared. Obviously it strongly supported the idea that Harry had dangled beside the bridge for a considerable length of time before dropping into the water. But what about the placement of the marks? Clearly Harry had not tied a rope around his neck and jumped, as he would have done if he were searching for a quick exit from this life. Harry had hung by a rope wrapped around his chest. It was almost as if his arms had been trapped, made useless, by the rope around him.

Point four: Harry's broken neck and fractured skull. They did not fit in as easily with the hanging concept, yet they did not invalidate it either. Once Harry fell into the raging river, presumably dead or near death, it would have been surprising if he hadn't crashed into a number of boulders and broken something.

Point five: the oil on Harry's fingers. The rope had oil on it, so it stood to reason that Harry's hands could have got some of it on them. But why was there oil on the rope? Marvin believed that he had hit upon the most important question of them all. He could feel it in his gut. The bridge had spots of oil on it, that was true—every road did. But most did not have *puddles* of oil on them. Yet this particular bridge just happened to have a large round oil *stain* in the center of it. Marvin glanced over his shoulder. By sheer coincidence—which he still did not believe in—the stain happened to be right behind where he was sitting. Directly out from where the remainder of the rope was tied under the bridge. As if there had once been a puddle there that had been absorbed into the wood.

Now what was the point of a puddle of oil on an open bridge?

Answer: None.

What was the use of a length of rope on a bridge? Answer: None.

Unless you wanted to make someone on a motorcycle go down.

Marvin was now sure he had it all figured out. At least he had a scenario that fit the facts. Harry Paster had learned the infamous Marvin Summer was going out with the pure and virginal Shelly Quade Friday night, November 12. He had also learned where they were going. Upset about the matter, possibly drunk as well, he had decided to rig a little surprise for the two lovebirds to run into on their way home. A rope stretched across a bridge at waist level in front of a motorcycle doing in excess of sixty miles an hour would play havoc with the driver of the bike, not to mention any passenger on the back.

Why would Harry pour out the oil when he had the rope to do the trick? The reason was clever. The police would find the oil when they found the bodies. They would not find the rope. It would be removed. The oil would be identified as the reason for their spill. Hit a slick at high speed and went down, the police report would say. It happened all the time on roads across the country.

Yet a portion of the rope was still attached to the bridge. Marvin held it in his hand. Plus Harry was dead—Shelly and he were alive. That could only mean something had gone wrong for Harry. Marvin believed he knew what it was. To carry out his plan Harry would have had to wait over the side of the bridge for them to come by. He couldn't have simply rigged the rope and left—the reason being that anyone who came by before them would take the rope on the chin, and if it was a car it would just snap it. No, Harry could only raise the rope as they were approaching. No doubt he would have been able to identify them from far off, flying over the hills like maniacs.

But waiting over the side of the bridge—that would have been tricky for anybody, even sober, which Marvin doubted Harry was. The side railings were old and rusted. Marvin could remember the night he had helped him celebrate Shelly's birthday. They hadn't started back from Pella until close to one in the morning. He could just see Harry out here waiting for them in the middle of the night, his hands numb, his heart hot, hanging on to the side of the bridge for dear life.

But, of course, that was a tiny bit wrong.

Because if Harry had had half a functioning brain left he wouldn't have depended on the railing alone to support him. He would have secured himself by—

Tying a rope around his waist!

Then what went wrong? It was simple.

Harry slipped and fell and hung himself. But it wasn't an ordinary hanging. Going by the marks on the jacket, the rope probably yanked up around his armpits and stuck there, unable to get past his shoulders. Harry would have slowly suffocated.

The bridge was wide. The river was loud. Harry might have hung there for days without anyone seeing or hearing him. Before dropping into the river and being washed into the lake. In fact, it might have taken him a couple of days to die. That would explain why the coroner set the time of Harry's death at early Monday morning.

Harry had not been murdered nor had he committed suicide. His death had most likely been an accident. To think the guy had been waiting to kill them.

Marvin stood from his lengthy analysis. He was convinced he was correct in his conclusion. He also suspected Shelly knew what he knew. What he didn't understand was where she was coming from now. What did she want with him? Why did she want to hurt him?

He thought of her in the Jacuzzi once more and shuddered.

Yet in a way he didn't care to know the answers to those last questions. After what he had seen that night he just wanted to hurt her. He glanced once more at the ragged end of rope, the old oil stain in the center of the bridge. Harry's plan had been a good one, even if it had cost him his life.

Marvin figured he could be more careful than Harry.

He smiled as he climbed onto his bike.

Those two were not going to be screwing Monday night.

CHAPTER 10

Marvin spent the rest of the night at a cheap motel in Pella. He could have afforded the most expensive lodging around but the squalor of the place fit his state of mind. There were spiders in the bathroom, ants in the mattress, and the mirror over the chest of drawers was cracked and covered with dust. Marvin slept the night in Harry's leather jacket. He was in a killer of a mood.

He awoke at ten in the morning when a cleaning lady banged on his door. Apparently at the discount rates you weren't allowed to sleep in. He stumbled out into the morning sun and had to shield his eyes from the glare. His head felt as if it were ready to split open. Just punching a drunk had given him a hangover. Fortunately no one had stolen his bike.

Fortunate because today was the day he was going to sell it.

But first, before he set his plan in motion, he would give her one last chance. He drove to a phone booth and called Shelly. She took a while to answer. She sounded sleepy. He wondered why.

"Hello?" she said.

"Hi," he said.

"Marvin?"

"That's the one. How are you doing?"

"I don't know. What time is it?"

"Ten-thirty," he said smoothly. "Want to have breakfast together?"

She yawned. "That's sweet, but I can't. I have stuff I have to do today."

"What kind of stuff?"

"Just stuff," she said. "Hey, where are you? It sounds like you're calling from a phone booth."

"I am. I have a favorite booth. I come here when I feel like turning into Superman."

She laughed softly. "You're funny."

"Yeah, I'm cool. Hey, where are we going tomorrow night?"

There was a long pause. He had expected it. What he had not expected was that he would enjoy it. "I'm sorry, Marvin," she said finally. "Tomorrow's no good."

He grinned. He could see his teeth reflecting in the glass wall of the phone booth. He looked like one happy guy. "What's wrong with it?" he asked.

"I have a cousin coming in from out of town. I had forgotten all about it when I promised you we could go out. I'm sorry."

121

"No problem," Marvin said. "We can always go out another time." He added, "I still want to talk to you about what I've found out about Harry."

"Sure." She didn't sound that enthusiastic. Only yesterday she had been crying on his shoulder about her poor dead boyfriend. Of course, right now she probably had Triad lumbering naked beside her. Marvin reminded himself that Triad and Harry had been good friends. The way Shelly got around made Ann McGaffer look like a nun. It was funny, though, how similar they were—in different ways. He hadn't really thought about it before.

"I've got Harry's jacket on," Marvin said.

"What?"

"His leather jacket. The one he died in. I'm wearing it."

She had to digest that remark. "Does it fit?"

"Perfectly. I've got to go, Shelly. You take care of yourself. Stay out of the cold." He hung up the phone before she could reply.

He would have to call Triad later, when the guy had recovered from his hours of lovemaking. Marvin drove back to the motel where he had stayed the past night and walked into the office with his helmet in his hands. The manager was at the front desk, a scruffy middle-aged man who looked as if he needed to shave off the last ten years of his life. Marvin had met him the night before. He smelled like the stale sheets in the rooms. He probably never left the place.

"I have a friend who's going to be picking up this helmet tonight," Marvin said, pulling a twenty-dollar bill out from his pocket. "If he calls first before he comes, tell him he's got to get it tonight, that you don't want to be responsible for it." Marvin handed the old guy the money. "Would that be all right?"

The man stared at the bill. "You're going to give me twenty bucks to watch a helmet for one day?"

"I promised my friend I would get it to him, but I'm leaving town. His name's Triad. He looks like a jock." Marvin added, "He's a real nice guy."

The deal was agreeable to the man. Next Marvin drove to a GM dealer in the heart of Pella. There was a gorgeous red Corvette in the showroom window. Marvin strolled in and asked the salesman how much it cost.

"Now hold on there, son," the guy said. His name was Ed, according to his tag. He was from Texas, Oklahoma, maybe—a big man with a loud mouth and a strangling handshake. "This is one fancy automobile for a boy like you to be thinking of owning."

"I can afford it," Marvin said.

Ed chuckled. "How do you know you can afford it if you don't know how much it costs?"

Marvin pulled his checkbook from his back pocket and tore out a check. "I'd be happy to let you see how much I have in my account. We can go to a cash machine and I'll get a printout of my balance." He handed the check to the man. "When you see, you'll know I don't care what the car costs. But I will want it today—delivered to a specific location in Sesa at four in the evening. I'll want the car left locked, but with the keys tucked inside the muffler."

Ed left with Marvin to check at a cash machine on Marvin's balance. When they returned, Ed was sufficiently humbled to give Marvin a test drive and the long version of the story of his life, which Ed thought would make a great book, but which Marvin knew wouldn't sell to a paper shredder. The Corvette Marvin had purchased was a special-edition and cost seventy-two thousand dollars. Marvin drew Ed a map showing where he wanted the car deposited. Ed wanted to know if Marvin had a rich daddy. Marvin gave him a cool smile.

Marvin drove to the mall in Pella next. The place would have opened at noon. He was feeling in a reckless mood. He tried eating a hamburger from McDonald's, but it made him think of dead cows. He had no appetite. He felt as if his nerves had been greased with blue lightning; he simply couldn't relax. He was not giving himself a chance to slow down and sort out what he was planning. He didn't want to. Harry had already done all the planning. Marvin just wanted to do it.

He was going to bring Triad down. Hard.

He would have felt guilty about the prospect if he hadn't felt so *good* about the end result. Triad laid out like a broken slab of beef on the bridge. That would sure put a dent in his love life. Nope, can't screw tonight, Shelly. I'm paralyzed from the neck down and they've got me attached to this heart-lung machine. Maybe you should call Marvin. I hear he's available.

Yes, Marvin thought, he would get to Shelly next.

Marvin wandered over to one of the bookstores.

The mall had two. In the teen section he found two girls about sixteen years old picking through his books. One was brunette, the other blond—both cute. They were gushing to each other about how fantastic Mack Slate was. Marvin stared at them for a minute before speaking.

"I know the guy who writes those books," he said.

The girls looked at him, and he could imagine what they saw. A smelly downbeat in a ruined leather coat with wild eyes. Yet they were curious.

"How do you know him?" the brunette asked.

"I used to live near him," Marvin said.

The blonde's eyes widened. "What's he like?"

Marvin shrugged. "He's a great guy. But he's not a snob. He never acts like he's better than anybody else."

"How old is he?" the brunette asked.

"Is he married?" the blonde asked.

"He's not that old," Marvin said. "You'd be amazed how young he is. He's not married."

"Does he have a girlfriend?" the blonde asked.

"He had one," Marvin said sadly. "But not now."

The girls glanced at each other uneasily, perhaps because of his sudden change in tone. "Do you know where he gets his ideas?" the brunette asked.

Marvin bowed his head. "Yeah. He looks around him at the horror in the world. All the pain people cause one another. And he writes about it." Marvin glanced up. "But don't get me wrong. He's a good person. He doesn't want to hurt anybody. But if he has to, if the story makes him do it, then he doesn't hesitate. He kills the girl and doesn't cry about it. He takes full responsibility. Do you know what I mean?"

Both girls were confused. "Do you know how we could write to him?" the blonde asked hesitantly.

Marvin straightened his shoulders. "Sure. I'll give you his address. Here, let me write it in his book so you don't lose it."

"I haven't bought that book yet," the blonde protested as he took it from her hands.

"It doesn't matter," Marvin said. He took a pen from his pocket and opened to the title page. *The Mystery of Silver Lake V: The Last Breath*. By Mack Slate. Marvin had never signed one of his books before. It made him sad—no one had ever asked him. "What's your name?" he asked the blonde.

She hesitated. "Marjorie."

He smiled. "Marjorie," he muttered. "I don't know if he would like me giving out his address, but I can give you something else."

Then he wrote.

> For Marjorie,
> You are beautiful.
>
> > Best Wishes,
> > Mack Slate

Marvin was still smiling when he handed the book back to the girl. But neither of them was happy to see what he had written.

"Why did you do that?" the brunette asked.

"You messed up the book," the blond girl complained. "I told you, it's not even mine."

"I am Mack Slate," Marvin said.

The brunette grabbed her friend's arm. "Come on, let's get away from this creep. Put that book back. You don't have to buy it."

"He should have to buy it," Marjorie snorted, sticking the book back on the shelf. Marvin quickly picked it back up.

"No, I'm serious," he said, blocking their way. "I really am Mack Slate. I didn't tell you at first because I didn't want you to get all excited."

The brunette dropped her mouth three inches and looked at him as if he were the year's winner of the "Lobotomites in Action" award. "We are not excited," she sneered. "We are pissed. And if you don't get out of our way, bozo, we're going to scream bloody murder."

"But I am Mack Slate," Marvin said. "I know all of his books inside out. Ask me anything."

"If you are Mack Slate," the brunette said, "then I am Madonna." She shoved him hard in the chest. "Go pick on some retarded chicks, pervert. Let's go, Marjorie."

Marvin took a step back and accidentally dropped his book on the floor. He knelt down to pick it up, his face beet red, and took his sweet time getting back up. He must have been out of his mind to pull a stunt like that, he thought. But of course that was exactly the case, because later in the night he was planning to kill a young man speeding along on a motorcycle.

Marvin was surprised to find the blonde standing beside him when he straightened up. Her friend had already gone for the manager of the store.

"What do you want?" he asked.

"Are you really Mack Slate?" Marjorie asked.

"Look, what did you expect? I'm a writer. I'm not an actor. I don't walk around looking brilliant. Yeah, I'm Mack Slate. I don't care if you believe me or not."

"Who killed Ann McGaffer?" Marjorie asked.

"You're reading the series?"

"Who isn't? Who killed her?"

Marvin closed his eyes and took a deep breath. He still had a headache. He still had Shelly moaning in Triad's arms inside his head. He reopened his eyes. The girl was watching him closely. She seemed worried about him. She wasn't such a bad sort, after all.

"I'm not sure," he said finally. "I'm still finishing the last book. It's possible no one killed her."

Marjorie winced. "Ann committed suicide?"

"I think her death might have been an accident." He raised his hand when she began to protest. "Like I said, I'm not sure about this. But if you are a fan of mine you must know that the facts are never what they appear to be. But there is one thing I can tell you. Ann did not die at the lake. She died on the bridge that crosses the river—the one that flows into the lake."

A spark of wonder ignited deep in the depths of Marjorie's eyes—the spark of belief. She nodded. "I guess we'll see, won't we?" She stuck out her hand. "Can I have my book back, Mr. Slate?"

He gave it to her. "Thank you," he muttered.

She hugged the book to her chest and smiled.

"Thank you for writing such great books. You're the best."

Marvin nodded grimly. "That's what they tell me."

It was only as he walked back to his motorcycle that he understood what he had told Marjorie. The mystery of Silver Lake was the mystery of his hometown. But he had already solved that mystery, he thought.

He could start writing the last book as soon as he killed Triad.

CHAPTER 11

"Hello, Triad? This is Marvin. How are you doing? That's great. Yeah, I bet. I was up late myself. We'll be old before we know it. Hey, I've got good news for you. I'm selling my bike. Do you want to buy it? Of course I'm going to rip you off. We'll work something out. Why don't I come over in an hour? That's good? Great. See ya."

Marvin set the phone down. They would see who the worm was.

Marvin had called from a phone booth outside a Sears. He was still in Pella, but was working his way slowly back toward Sesa. Before he left the booth he debated calling Ann to make sure she was okay and to assure her that he had not gone off the deep end during the night. The problem was he had gone off the deep end, and he had yet to hit the ground. He decided to talk to her later, when his mind was clearer.

Marvin walked into the Sears. His shopping list was short and he was able to get all the items he needed right there: a hundred feet of rope, a quart of oil, a pair of binoculars, and a knife. No one gave him a suspicious look.

Many times in his novels he had described how a murderer felt before committing a wicked deed, but none of his killers had ever felt the way he did now. He moved as if in a dream. The most amazing thing was that he didn't consider his plan evil. It was almost as if he were doing his duty. Yet he realized that whatever joy the task gave him came from the fact that Triad was sleeping with the love of his life. That fact gave him strength.

He didn't drive straight to Triad's after leaving the Sears. He drove around for a while and then went to see if his Corvette was waiting where it was supposed to be, in a parking lot around the block from Triad's house. Ed had kept his word. The red car was there, glistening in the afternoon light. Marvin didn't know how he was going to explain it to his mother, and frankly, he didn't care. He pulled the keys from the tail pipe and stowed his purchases in the trunk. He didn't want Triad to see them.

Triad was outside tinkering with a snowblower, getting it ready for winter, when Marvin drove up on his bike. Triad had on his usual puppy-dog grin and it was all Marvin could do not to take a wrench out of Triad's tool kit and break his teeth with it. But Triad did not totally lack in perception. The first question out of his mouth brought a smile to Marvin's lips.

"Hey, where's your helmet?" Triad asked. "Aren't you going to throw that in?"

"You have a bigger head than I do," Marvin said, climbing off his bike.

"Let's see." Triad measured the space between his ears with his open palms. Attempting to keep them the same distance apart, he moved them toward Marvin. Marvin brushed Triad's hands aside.

"You don't have to do that," he said. "It'll fit you. But I left my helmet in a cheap motel in Pella called the Slumber Bin. It's on Main Street, west of the mall. You'll have to pick it up tonight if you want it. I called the manager. He's going to throw it out or take it home unless somebody gets it tonight."

Marvin was not worried that the manager would have a different story to tell Triad. Triad wasn't going to be talking about it to anybody.

"What were you doing there?" Triad asked.

"That's where I spent the night."

Triad was interested. "Get any?"

"Got more than I could handle." Marvin patted the handlebars of his bike. That was the worst thing wrong with the scheme. He was going to ruin his lovely wheels. Well, it couldn't be helped. When you fought a war you always lost some artillery. "So what are you going to give me for this speed machine?"

Triad gave him what he probably thought was a sly grin, but which Marvin interpreted to be the confused expression of a buffoon. "How about five hundred dollars?" he asked.

"How about twice that?" Marvin asked.

"I don't have twice that."

"Why don't you go inside and ask Mommy for a little change."

"My mom's not home."

"Then take it out of her cookie jar. You can't have the bike for five hundred bucks."

"How about eight hundred?" Triad asked.

Marvin paused. "All right."

Triad was surprised, and did a poor job of hiding it. He stuck out his fat hand. "Deal," he exclaimed.

Marvin looked down at the open hand with revulsion. Yet he shook it with pleasure. "It's a deal," Marvin said.

Triad ran into the house and got his checkbook —or his mother's as it turned out. Marvin had the pink registration slip in his wallet and signed it over. Marvin reminded him about the helmet and Triad promised he'd get it right after dinner. He even offered Marvin a ride home. But Marvin declined.

"I need the exercise," he said.

"But your house is on the other side of town."

"Who cares?" Marvin turned away. "Don't kill yourself on the bike."

"If I do, I'll take plenty with me," Triad called after him.

CHAPTER 12

Marvin walked back to the Corvette and sat in his car for a long time and did nothing else. The leather upholstery was soft; it smelled nice. The steering was snug, but not too tight. It occurred to Marvin that he had been wearing Harry's jacket when he had made his deal with Triad and Triad hadn't even noticed.

Marvin was beginning to get the feeling there was something he was missing. He reviewed his analysis of what he had envisioned had happened the previous year, but could find no flaw. Harry *must* have been after revenge. He *must* have accidentally hung himself. All the evidence supported the scenario Marvin had developed—it didn't support any other he could think of.

Yet Marvin knew he was operating with major

blind spots. He still didn't know why Shelly had drawn him into the details of Harry's death. He didn't know who was sending him the letters. He didn't know why he had changed overnight from a mild-mannered mystery writer to a bloodthirsty teenager. But then he thought of Triad and Shelly together in the Jacuzzi—he simply couldn't stop the images from returning, again and again. And all he wanted to do was get back at them.

What had he told the girl in the bookstore? Ann McGaffer had died the same way Harry Paster had died? Had he been rambling? No, the connection was clear now that he knew Harry had not committed suicide. But he hadn't known that when he'd started on his series. He could swear he hadn't.

But *when* had he started the series?

Hadn't it been a couple of weeks after they buried Harry?

Hadn't he dropped another book to write it?

God. He had started on it like a man possessed.

Why had he written it?

No more questions. No answers.

Just kill the bastard and be done with it.

"It doesn't matter," Marvin whispered to himself. "I'll finish it tonight."

Sitting behind the luxurious wheel of his new car Marvin began to doze. The parking lot where he sat was empty—the store was closed for Sunday. But he would not let himself sleep. He was afraid if he slept he'd dream. He remembered then the dream he'd been having when his father had come over. He realized his subconscious had been trying to alert him to the fact of Harry's death by showing him Ann McGaffer in an identical position. It may have been the dream that had allowed him to solve the mystery so quickly. Yet had the dream told him anything new besides how Harry had died? He could have sworn there were a couple of parts in there that hadn't been in his manuscripts. He probably should get those books out again and study them. He never really did read his own work—not once it was printed.

His subconscious. His muse. His rage. His broken heart.

What was the difference between any of them?

I'm going to kill that bastard. Then I'll get her. Somehow.

Marvin shook himself into an upright position. He'd get something to eat before he headed for the bridge. It might be the last meal he enjoyed as an innocent man.

A couple hours later, cloaked in the darkness of a night so black it could have been made for crime, Marvin slowed his shiny Corvette on the road a mile before the Pella Bridge. It was exactly 6:26, and he had a small problem. He had no idea when Triad would go to Pella and it was too cold a night to hang on to the side of a bridge for several hours. What if he set up his rope and oil right now and Triad didn't decide to go to Pella until after ten at night? His body would be so frozen he wouldn't have the strength to pull up the rope in front of Triad. Marvin briefly wondered if that was what had happened to Harry. If that was how the guy had accidentally killed himself. Marvin could remember how cold it had been last year on Shelly's birthday.

Like tonight. Everything was like tonight.

Marvin was reasonably certain Triad had not already passed him on the road to Pella. Triad had said he'd eat first before he went for the helmet. Marvin decided the best course of action would be to wait until Triad crossed the bridge before setting up his rope. He would get Triad later, when Triad was on the way back. That way he wouldn't have to wait out in the cold forever. Also, there would be less traffic on the road at a later hour. Not that there was ever much after sunset.

Marvin pulled his car off the side and parked behind a tree that was over a hundred yards from the edge of the road. He wanted to be sure he wasn't spotted. He killed the engine and the lights. He would have liked to leave the engine running so he could keep the heat on, but feared someone would notice, and later report to the police that there had been a suspicious vehicle in the area the night the football player crashed on the bridge.

Seven o'clock came, followed by eight and nine, and still no sign of Triad. The heat seeped out of the car and left Marvin shivering in the front seat in Harry's leather jacket. Marvin began to despair that Triad was ever going to drive by, yet he didn't consider for a moment leaving and going home. He had the patience of an obsessed man, which he thought was an apt word for his condition. He spent the cold hours remembering his last date with Shelly last year—before Harry died.

It had been a night of magic for Marvin. When he

had picked her up at home she had greeted him at the door with a smile that he was never to forget. Because he thought he saw in it her love. Yeah, he thought she was falling for him, the way he was falling for her. Such a simple thing, he knew. It happened all over the world between couples. But it had never happened to him before, and because she was his first he wanted her to be his last as well. He considered asking her to marry him right then. He was already a successful author, long before his series appeared. He could have supported her. He would have done anything for her.

They went to dinner and ate their food by candlelight. They went to a show and ate popcorn. They drove home at ninety miles an hour on his bike, and they didn't see or feel any rope as they flew over the bridge. He could remember her laughing in his ear—her happiness. Her parents had been away for that weekend as well, and he had kissed her on her bed until four in the morning, not knowing that all the while Harry was hanging by a rope above an icy river. Shelly had not spoken of Harry once that night. In fact, just as he was leaving her, at the end of their last kiss, she had whispered in his ear that this was what she wanted, that she didn't want anyone else.

And he had believed her.

Until Monday. A body found floating in the lake. Blue Monday.

Why? he kept asking himself. Why had she turned a cold shoulder to him when Harry died? Why if it was really him she loved? Of course, the answer was painfully simple. She could say and do anything. She didn't love him. She had proven that to him the previous night when he had caught her in Triad's arms.

Yet . . . there was something he was missing. Something about her.

Something he was seeing but not understanding.

Marvin sat up in his seat.

He could hear a motorcycle in the distance. Approaching swiftly from the direction of Sesa. He reached for his binoculars, before remembering he had left them in the trunk. He cursed silently, although he knew he didn't really need them. He was far from the road and it was as black as it got, but he didn't need to see Triad to know for sure it was him. Who knew the sound of that bike better than he did? He just had to wait until the bike came a little closer.

A couple of minutes later he knew Triad had fallen for his bait. The motorcycle roared by Marvin's hiding spot at a hysterical speed and the sound of its pistons was sweet music to Marvin's ears. Really, he told himself, in his next book he must make it so that his villain enjoyed doing in his victim. There was no reason a murder mystery had to be gloomy.

When Triad had passed, Marvin climbed out of his car and stood for a few minutes in the frozen air, watching the solitary headlight disappear over the distant hills. It was eight miles to Pella from the river, maybe ten to the actual motel. Triad would be back in half an hour if he didn't loiter in town.

Marvin doubted he would. There was school the next day, and then Shelly at night. Triad would probably want to go straight back to bed.

Marvin decided to leave his car where it was and walk to the bridge. There were few trees between where he was parked and the river. It would be disastrous if Triad spotted him at the last instant—after he had set up the rope. He could go to jail . . . Triad could kill him—neither a fun prospect. Besides, Marvin thought, he should walk and warm up. He grabbed his rope, the knife, the oil, and the binoculars and headed toward the road. It was 9:44. Triad's motorcycle had been the last vehicle to go by for over an hour. Marvin doubted anyone would drive by until Triad returned. He reached the road and started toward the bridge.

The hike to the river took him close to twenty minutes, longer than he expected. Now he had to work quickly. The exercise had done little to get his blood pumping. Indeed, as he knelt and began to tie his rope to the railing at the north end of the bridge, he felt colder than he had in the Corvette. He didn't have his gloves and it was hard to make a respectable knot with his fingers on the verge of going numb. His task was doubly complicated. He had to make his knot strong, but he had to be able to untie it in seconds. There was always the remote possibility somebody could come by right after Triad went down. Marvin had never been a Boy Scout; he didn't know much about slipknots and stuff like that, even though the characters in his books used them a time or two.

Marvin didn't tie his rope where Harry had positioned his, but put it much closer to the Pella side of the bridge. He didn't want the police to find Harry's evidence and connect it with Triad's accident. Indeed, Marvin thought, when he was done, if there was time, it might not be a bad idea to get rid of what was left of Harry's rope. Still, there was plenty of rushing water beneath the spot where Marvin would have to wait for Triad. If he slipped, if he fell, the last book in his series would never get written.

Marvin had a lot more rope than he needed, but decided against cutting it, which was the reason he had purchased the knife. He wanted to keep his instruments of death as together as possible. Before wrapping his rope around the opposite rail, he opened his easy-to-pour can of oil. He put his puddle just beyond the spot where Triad would hit the rope, and made it wide, eight feet across the center of the bridge. Marvin knew he didn't need his rope to be in the exact spot the puddle was. Triad would slide into the oil—of that there was no doubt. Marvin didn't want to get oil on his rope for the simple reason that he was going to take the rope with him when he left and he didn't want to get stains on his new car.

Now came the hard part. He had to go over the side of the railing with his end of the rope and keep both the rope and himself out of sight. Besides, there was always the slim possibility that at the last instant Triad would glimpse the rope in his headlight and swerve in time to avoid doing himself serious damage. Therefore, as Marvin had already figured, he had to raise the rope just before Triad crossed the bridge.

But now he was faced with the dilemma that had done Harry in. The only safe way to hang over the side of the bridge was to secure himself with the rope. A sudden gust of wind—and it was already very windy—could jolt his freezing fingers free and send him spiraling down into a cruel bath. The best thing to do was what Harry had done—wrap the rope around the railing once and then tie it around his own waist. Marvin hesitated to follow in his mentor's footsteps because, after all, the guy had ended up killing himself. Yet he could see no better way. He consoled himself that he wasn't an uncoordinated duck as Harry had been.

Except Harry had been an excellent athlete.

And still he had died.

Marvin tried not to think about it. He'd be careful.

He wrapped the rope around the railing. Around his waist.

Talk about scary.

The trouble with Pella Bridge was that it should have been condemned. Time and traffic had done a number on the splintered boards and the rusty beams. Marvin heard the railing groan as he swung his leg over the side, and Marvin himself groaned when he had both legs over and was looking down. The river roared in his ears like the Abominable Snowman. The water looked like black foam gushing from a hole that had no bottom. The spray touched his face, his ears, and sent a shiver that reached inside his chest. For a moment he wondered what the hell he was doing.

But he was not unhappy.

In fact, he felt strangely exhilarated.

Marvin crouched down on the planks that made up the lower level of the bridge. They were longer than the boards that made up the upper layer; they therefore protruded above the water and provided him with a questionable place to wait. If Triad looked directly his way, however, as he crossed the bridge, he would see Marvin. But Marvin had never looked to the right or the left as he had gone over the water and he doubted Triad would do any differently.

It was only in the last minutes that Marvin asked himself exactly what the rope would do to Triad. The impact would yank him off his bike surely, but would it kill him? Marvin doubted the rope itself would touch Triad. He had set the rope at handlebar level, lest the rope leave a mark on Triad's chest that would cause the county coroner to probe deeper than an oil spill. Not that the coroner had impressed Marvin as a clever investigator.

What would happen to Triad when he hit the bridge? All along Marvin had assumed that it would kill him, but now he wasn't sure. Triad would be returning from Pella with his helmet on. The helmet could take a hard pounding before it shattered. Marvin had taken a couple of nasty spills on the bike—while wearing the helmet—and had been able to walk away from them with nothing more than badly skinned knees. Of course, those falls had been at speeds more in the thirty-mile-an-hour range. Triad would be doing at least sixty, maybe more, when he hit the bridge. Plus his fall would be instantaneous. He would be snapped back and pinned hard by the demon of momentum. Yeah, the more Marvin thought about it the more unlikely it seemed that Triad would survive with enough brain cells left to be called human.

If he ever deserved the name.

Right then, far away, Marvin heard the sound.

A motorcycle with an engine revved high.

Coming from the direction of Pella.

Marvin caught a glimpse of light in the hills. He reached for his binoculars, which were slung around his neck like a loosened tie, and which so far had caused him more trouble than they were worth. With the wind they kept banging against his chest. By this time—and he hadn't been waiting long over the side of the railing, maybe five minutes—his fingers felt like ice crystals. He grabbed the binoculars only to lose them again. He must not have checked that the neck strap was fastened when he bought them. The binoculars slipped out of his hands, bounced on his knees, and toppled into the river.

"Christ," Marvin whispered.

He felt upset for a moment but then realized he didn't need the binoculars. The chance of another motorcycle coming from Pella at this exact time was remote. Plus he could always reconfirm it was Triad by the sound of the bike, as he had done when Triad had passed by a half hour ago.

Maybe. It would be harder to distinguish the

specific sound of the engine over the roar of the water.

"It's him," Marvin said to himself. "It's got to be him."

The faint glow in the hills grew into a powerful headlight as Triad wound his way out of the hills and hit the straight mile stretch that led directly to the bridge. He was going fast, Marvin thought, at least sixty, maybe seventy, seventy-five. The glare of the headlight reached Marvin's eyes and his grip on the rope tightened. Naturally he had left the rope lax across the width of the bridge, and around the bar of the railing, but now slowly he began to pull it taut. He realized right then that he would be unable to snap the rope up on Triad in the last second as he had planned. He would have to do it several seconds before Triad got to the bridge if he was to have time to tie off his loop around the railing so that his own waist did not take the impact of the yank. He realized something else right then as well. The snap of the rope might yank the railing loose and leave behind evidence of foul play that would be impossible to remove. Indeed, the rope might yank his guts out.

Now why hadn't Mr. Master of Murder thought of that before?

Reality was much more complicated than pretend.

Still, Marvin remained committed.

He pulled the rope taut.

He secured it around the railing.

It stretched like a dark knife in the night.

Triad was coming.

Half a mile away. Thirty seconds.

And still Marvin was committed.

Twenty seconds.

Because he could still see them groaning in each other's arms.

Quarter of a mile away. Fifteen seconds.

Because he had told her he loved her.

The roar of the engine.

Two hundred yards.

And she had told him she loved him.

The glare of the headlight. Blinding.

One hundred yards. Four seconds. Less.

Because she had lied to him.

But could he really kill someone?

Could he?

He doubted it. Especially if it was someone he loved.

"Shelly!" Marvin screamed.

It was Triad but he had Shelly on the back. In a grotesque glimpse of light and shadow Marvin saw that Triad, and not Shelly, was wearing the helmet. Perhaps his scream alerted them; he couldn't be sure. Maybe Triad or Shelly saw the rope. In any case, Marvin frantically reached to loosen the rope and drop it to the bridge as Triad slammed on the motorcycle brakes and sent the bike into a dangerous slide. Burning rubber screeched over the roar of the river. As Marvin watched, the rear wheel of the bike crept steadily forward until it was almost in front of the front wheel. It occurred to him that Triad was no amateur when it came to riding a motorcycle—that Triad was in fact stopping the machine like an expert.

"Shelly!" Marvin shouted. Yes, in that moment, when time was suspended by the insane collection of colliding events, Marvin felt nothing but fear that Shelly, *his* Shelly, would be hurt.

But he should have saved his fear for himself.

Triad brought the bike to a halt two feet before the rope, but by then the rope was lying harmlessly on the ground.

The insane moments were not over, however.

Oh, no, they were just beginning.

"Son of a bitch!" Triad shouted as he brought the bike back into an upright position and turned off the engine. The stink of fried rubber filled the air. Triad snapped down the kickstand and leapt off the bike. He left the headlight on, however, pointed almost directly at Marvin, who was no longer crouching beneath the rail but standing upright on what he was beginning to realize was the very wrong side of the fence. Shelly got off the bike more leisurely, apparently unfazed by all the commotion. She moved with inexplicable weariness. Such could not be said for Triad, however. He threw off his helmet and stormed Marvin as if he intended to knock him off the side of the bridge.

Which, it turned out, was precisely his intention.

"You tried to kill us, you bastard!" Triad swore as he grabbed a dazed Marvin by the front of Harry's leather coat and lifted him off his feet.

"No," Marvin said.

Maybe his word lacked conviction. Triad didn't

seem to hear it. His face was a mask of ugly lines. Marvin didn't get to examine it closely though. Triad drew back his fist.

"You're dead meat," Triad spat.

The fist flew toward Marvin's face.

Marvin ducked. The fist missed his face.

Thank God, Marvin thought. He still had his teeth, his good looks. But he realized he should have at least waited until he was on solid ground to do his thanking. As Triad fought to recover his balance from his missed blow, he let go of Marvin. Or more exactly, he dropped Marvin. Off the side of the bridge.

Marvin hardly had time to register the fact that he was falling toward the river when he was stopped by a horrible yank. Pain shot through the length of his body as he bobbled in the dark like a marionette with a drunk for a puppeteer. He still had the rope wrapped around his waist. But it was moving fast, from under his armpits over the outsides of his arms. He saw that in a moment he would slip out of the rope and fall in the river. He had not tied it as tightly as Harry must have tied his for fear he would accidently hang himself by his armpits, as Harry had. Now he prayed he could hang on for a few seconds longer. He reached up with his right hand and grabbed the length of rope attached to the railing ten feet above him. Triad's big head stuck over the side. He was smiling.

"You're still there, huh?" Triad asked. He casually picked at the knot in the rope. "Not for long, sucker."

Sucker. He called me a sucker.

Had he been suckered?

"Triad, wait!" Marvin shouted.

Triad chuckled. "For what? You tried to kill us. That's a capital offense. You have to pay for it. You have to die."

"Stop it," Shelly said as she also appeared. The glare of the headlight illumined the side of her face and once more Marvin was struck by how weary her expression was. It was as if nothing unusual had happened to her this wildest of all nights. Just the same old rope-across-the-bridge trick. That Marvin, she could have been thinking. When would he ever learn?

"Shelly," Marvin said, and he hated the pleading note in his voice almost as much as he hated the raging water fifty feet below his dangling feet. He managed to take hold of the rope and pull himself up a foot, momentarily easing the tension on the lasso choking his upper body. Another few feet and he would be able to grab the edge of the boards he had been crouching on only moments ago. But even as he clung to the rope he felt it slipping slowly from his grasp. Plus Triad had not stopped fiddling with the knot. One thing their expressions had in common was disgust.

Yet neither looked surprised.

"I'm going to drop him now," Triad said. "Let him drown. It'll save everybody a lot of trouble."

"No, I said," Shelly snapped as she shoved Triad's hands off the rope. Marvin took the opportunity of their disagreement to hoist himself up another foot. Triad took a step back from the railing, but didn't move so far Marvin could no longer see him. Now, finally, Triad looked surprised.

"You want to save him after what he's tried?" Triad asked.

Shelly continued to stare down at Marvin. Such loathing in her eyes—Marvin felt like a worm crawling beneath her raised foot. But wasn't that what they had called him the night before, even before he had tried to harm them?

Even before. Curious. Very.

They set me up. Somehow they set me up.

They had known he would be at the bridge.

The muscles in his arms burned with fatigue.

"He's not going anywhere," Shelly said.

"I want him dead," Triad said.

Shelly glanced at Triad as if he were a minor annoyance. But Marvin was seeing Triad as a major red alert and he believed he was seeing things about the guy he'd never noticed before—things that Triad had carefully buried. Maybe his stark terror had heightened his sensitivity. But Marvin could have sworn there wasn't a trace of the usual puppy-dog innocence in Triad's face.

Meanwhile Marvin experiences a leap in consciousness and finds Clyde out drinking with his best friend, Terry Rogers. Clyde is telling Terry what a bitch Ann has become and Terry encourages Clyde to dump Ann while the dumping is good. But Marvin can see that Terry is only telling Clyde this because he wants Ann for himself.

In Silver Lake, everyone is screwing everyone else.

In Sesa. It was the same old story.

It *was* the same story.

A leap in consciousness. That's what his analysis had been missing.

Marvin wondered if Triad's innocence had ever been real.

"Don't be ridiculous," Shelly said to Triad. "We're not killing anybody. We're going to the police."

"The police." Triad snorted, and he wasn't happy. He was outright furious. Shelly couldn't see it because she was too preoccupied staring down at him, Marvin realized. A shadow of disappointment touched her weary expression.

"You're so predictable," she said.

"I'm sorry," Marvin replied. He reached up another foot and grabbed the edge of the planks he had been standing on while he had been waiting for the motorcycle. With the headlight in their faces he doubted they knew his exact predicament. But his arms were exhausted, on the verge of giving out. If he was going to do something he was going to have to do it soon.

"I would have thought Mack Slate could have come up with another scheme," Shelly said sarcastically.

"You know who I am?" Marvin asked.

She was bitter. "I know you."

Marvin gasped for breath. He couldn't hang here all night! "You think I killed Harry?" he asked.

Shelly nodded. "I suspected you had. But now I know—"

"Then why don't you just let him drop?" Triad interrupted. He wasn't really asking because he didn't wait for an answer. He grabbed hold of the rope. Shelly shoved his hands aside once more but this time Triad shoved her back. She momentarily disappeared from Marvin's view, only to reappear, her face flushed with anger.

"We're not killing him!" she yelled. "Then we'll be as rotten as he is. Let go of that knot! We have to pull him up!"

"Fat chance, sister," Triad replied, and now he wore a maniacal grin. It was a grin Marvin had seen a hundred times before and never understood. That was the problem with innocence and insanity— they walked the same narrow edge of reason, or lack of reason. But Marvin could now see that Triad had gone over the edge long ago.

There was no reason that Triad couldn't have helped Harry in his plot to get Marvin. Helped him so well that it backfired in Harry's face.

"He killed Harry!" Marvin cried.

Shelly briefly forgot her anger at her coconspirator. She burst out laughing. "Then why was it you who was the one waiting out here in the middle of the night with your piece of rope and your can of oil?" she asked.

"Because you put me out here," Marvin said with his own bitterness. "You knew I'd figure out how Harry died. But that was where you were wrong. That's where we both were wrong. You thought I killed Harry. I thought he killed himself. But look at your new boyfriend, Shelly. Look closely. Who's trying to kill who?"

There was power in his words because, finally, he was speaking the truth, even if he didn't, as of yet, realize exactly what Triad had done to Harry.

Shelly took a step back and cast an uneasy glance at Triad. Triad hardly noticed—he was too preoccupied with undoing the knot in the rope.

"I told you I want you to stop that," she said.

"Go to hell," Triad muttered.

"If you kill him the police will arrest you," Shelly said.

Triad whirled on her. "There will be no police! Nobody will know! It's done! You set it up and I'm finishing it!"

Shelly looked worried. "What are you talking about? Marvin did what I thought he would. He acted just like he did before when he got jealous. We've got proof now. We can clear Harry's name."

Triad almost choked at the mention of his friend. "Harry's name! Harry's fame! Who gives a damn? Harry's dead. He's better off dead. He was happy when it ended. I made sure he was happy. He took you and he didn't give a damn what I thought. No one gives a damn what I think."

Shelly was very worried now. She began to back up slowly. "I don't understand what you're saying, Triad. We made a plan. We have to stick to our plan. Marvin is—"

"Marvin is right," Triad cackled. And in a blur of speed and power he reached out and grabbed Shelly by the throat. He yanked her toward him until her face was inches from his steaming lips. "Marvin is a goddamm genius," Triad confided to Shelly.

"No!" Shelly screamed, throwing her head back and trying to shake loose. No such luck. Triad started training for football season the day after the previous football season ended. He lifted weights and injected himself with steroids and probably ate his hamburger raw. He was strong. He shifted his hold on Shelly to the back of her neck and smashed her forehead onto the railing. Shelly crumpled to the ground like a broken doll. Triad turned back to Marvin.

"I never read any of your goddamm books!" he growled.

"I bet you can't even read!" Marvin shouted back at him.

It may have been a bad time to insult Triad's intelligence. The glare from the motorcycle headlight had not fooled Triad's eyes one bit. Before he worked any more on the knot, he reached a powerful leg over the side of the railing and trounced on Marvin's clinging fingers. Marvin's fingers were about as cold as they could be and still have a trace of feeling left in them. That trace greatly magnified when Triad's heel ground into his knuckles. Marvin screamed and let go of the planks.

God!

He did not fall exactly as he had a minute before. This time he had seen the attack coming and instinctively jerked back from Triad just before Triad stepped on his fingers. The jerking motion caused him to swing out, away from the bridge, as he snapped at the end of his short line. But when an object is swung one way on the end of a rope, it has to swing back the other way. Marvin caught a glimpse of Triad returning to the knot before his momentum carried him under the bridge.

It was dark under there. Marvin couldn't see anything and immediately whacked his head on a

154

board. He shot out his arms and grabbed the offensive piece of wood with both hands. He praised it rather than cursed it when he felt the tension on the rope suddenly disappear. Triad had finished undoing the knot. Marvin felt the remainder of the rope, the part that had been stretched across the bridge, whip down toward the water.

That was when he had his first good idea of the entire night.

"Ah!" Marvin screamed.

But it was no ordinary scream. It was a carefully formulated trick. He let it trail off swiftly, and then suddenly stop, as if he had gone into the water. Then he became completely silent. He hung under the bridge with the muscles in his arms crying for relief and his lungs bursting for air and didn't utter a peep.

"Hello?" Triad shouted. "Marvin?"

Yeah, like I'm really going to shout back, "Over here, Triad. Come kill me. It's getting late."

Then Triad did the most amazingly stupid thing. He had to be complimented for not completely falling for Marvin's fake plunge; that was true. But there was no excusing him when he got down on his belly and pulled himself a couple of feet under the railing so that he could lean over to see if Marvin was holding on to the bottom of the bridge. The fact that Marvin was doing exactly that still didn't get Triad off the hook. Because as soon as Triad stuck his head over the edge and peeked under the bridge he placed his face in a perfect position for a major rearrangement courtesy of the heel of Marvin's right boot.

"Hi," Marvin said when he saw Triad's surprised expression. Marvin swung up and kicked as he had never kicked in his life. His first blow caught Triad smack on the nose and made a sickening cracking sound. A wad of blood burst over Triad's face as if it had been waiting inside a delicate balloon attached to his cheek. Triad's head rolled forward and went limp but that didn't stop Marvin. He swung up once more and kicked the top of Triad's head, causing the football player's fat neck to snap back.

Marvin might have kicked him a third and fourth time if it hadn't been for the fact that his arms simply couldn't take any more. Desperately he clawed his way back to the edge of the bridge. In this effort he was aided by the fact that the bottom of the bridge was crisscrossed by easy-to-grab boards. In a moment he was hanging beside Triad's messy face. The guy was still breathing.

Worse, he appeared to be coming around.

"Damn," Marvin muttered. He would have to back up the way he had come to get in position to kick Triad again—if he had the strength, which he did not. No, he thought, he had to get back on top of the bridge or else he was going to fall in the water whether Triad put him there or he did.

Marvin took a deep breath and pivoted in midair and raised a clawing hand, groping for anything that would support his weight. Of all things—he got Triad's belt buckle. What the hell, he thought. The guy was heavy. He was wedged in the lower part of the railing. If Triad couldn't support him then they would both drown and so be it.

"One more second, that's all I ask, arms," Marvin muttered.

He pulled himself up. He almost gave himself two hernias and a stroke in the process. But he sure felt good when he was sitting on the bridge, catching his breath. He felt like a million dollars—no, two. He had, after all, almost that much in the bank.

He felt that way for maybe five seconds.

That was when Triad sat up and looked at him with bloodshot eyes. "Where the hell did you come from?" Triad asked, dazed.

Marvin leapt to his feet and slammed his heel down on the side of Triad's left knee, which was hanging over his right leg at a precarious angle. Something metallic clanged on the road as Marvin attacked, but he didn't take the time to look down to see what it was. There was cruel design to Marvin's blow. Triad had hurt his left knee the previous season and had had surgery on it after the last game. Triad howled at the kick and doubled his knee up to his chest.

"You are dead meat," Triad swore, grimacing.

"You said that already and I'm still kicking," Marvin replied. But he didn't immediately try to press his advantage. He appeared to have briefly crippled Triad, but the guy had at least twice his strength even stretched out like a beached whale on the boards. He was debating what to do next when Shelly began to come around. Marvin was both relieved to see that she had not fractured her skull open and disgusted that she had chosen that exact second to sit up.

"Marvin," she muttered when she saw him standing in the beam of the headlight. She raised an unsteady hand to her eyes to shield them from the glare. "Where's Triad?"

Triad, of course, was sitting only three feet to her right. Triad snarled in response to her remark and reached out and grabbed her by the mane of her long brown hair and dragged her to his side. Shelly let out a painful shriek. For a moment Triad tried to use her as a crutch to help him stand up, but Shelly was not as easy to handle as a piece of furniture. Triad's left leg crumpled as soon as he put weight on it. But the football player was tough. He continued to hang on to Shelly, who was now fully awake and whacking him fiercely.

"Let me go, you bastard!" she swore.

"Sure," Triad said. He drew back his hand and slapped her across the face. The noise from the blow made Marvin wince; still, he didn't immediately go to Shelly's aid. Shelly's head wobbled on her neck for a moment but she didn't lose consciousness. Blood seeped from her nose as she glared at Triad.

"You're the one," she said bitterly.

Triad gripped her tighter. "Hold still," he said.

"Better let her go," Marvin said. He was delighted at how he had managed to turn the tables on them and solve the mystery all in the space of five minutes. But they were at a dangerous stalemate, which was made doubly dangerous when Triad's eyes flashed on the knife lying on the bridge near his injured leg. Marvin saw it at the same instant. It was *his* knife—the one he had bought at Sears. It must have bounced from his pocket when he crunched Triad's knee.

They both went for the blade, but Triad had only to reach over and pick it up—it was no contest.

"Stop," Triad said to Shelly as he raised the knife to her throat. She was a spunky girl, but she was no dummy. She became perfectly still as the blade pressed against her skin. Marvin backed off a couple of steps.

"You are scum," Shelly whispered through chattering teeth. The cold wind continued to howl. Triad surveyed the scene and smiled.

"I want you to wheel the bike over to me," Triad said to Marvin.

"And if I don't?" Marvin asked.

"If you don't," Triad said, and he poked Shelly just enough to prick her skin and send a red streak running down the front of her pale neck. "I will slit her throat open."

Marvin considered for a moment. "All right," he said.

Triad blinked. "All right what?"

"Slit her throat open," Marvin said.

Triad chuckled. "I'm not bluffing."

"I'm not either." Marvin casually picked up the helmet Triad had thrown down when he had stormed to the railing and placed it over his head. He began to readjust the strap. He checked the time on his watch. "I'm going home to take a warm bath," he said.

"Marvin," Shelly moaned.

"Yes, Shelly?" Marvin asked. "What can I do for you?"

Her eyes were wide. She was scared. He would have been with a blade that sharp pressed to his throat. "Save me," she said pitifully.

"I'll do it, Marvin," Triad swore. "I'll open your lady love up like a piece of meat."

"I don't mind," Marvin said.

Both Triad and Shelly were shocked.

"You can't just leave," she complained.

"You can't take my bike," Triad said.

Marvin finished readjusting the strap on his helmet. He strode over to the motorcycle and swung his leg over the seat. Triad had left the key in the ignition.

"But I can," Marvin said. He booted the kickstand up and started the engine. The Corvette was nice, but it felt good to have his old wheels beneath him. His fingers were stiff from when Triad had stepped on them but not so stiff that he couldn't crank the throttle. The roar of the bike mingled with that of the wind and water. Marvin felt a strange relief inside—one he hadn't known in a long time.

"He'll kill me," Shelly cried.

"I'll kill her," Triad agreed.

Marvin smiled. "I'll tell you what Mack Slate would say about this situation. He would say that it was BS. The heroine sets the hero up, but now she wants him to rescue her. But he doesn't have the motivation, you see. He doesn't care if the villain kills her. Then there's the villain himself. He's as bad off as the heroine. He doesn't know that he's already blown it. He can't kill the heroine because then the hero will tell the police. He can't kill the hero because he can't get to him. The villain may as well kill himself. Or here's a better idea. The heroine should try to kill the villain. The guy's rotten to the core and it would give the heroine a chance to redeem herself—if that's possible."

There were tears on Shelly's face. "How can she do it?" she asked.

For a moment Marvin's cool demeanor wavered. A pretty face could do that to a guy—certainly to him. But the last couple of days had taught him what a pretty face could hide. His resolve strengthened.

"There's always a way," Marvin said.

He drove away. He left them on the bridge, at each other's throats, in the middle of the cold night. His conscience was clear. He hadn't hurt anybody. He couldn't worry about everything. He had things to do. He had a book to write.

CHAPTER 13

Marvin did not go home. He did stop at his car, however, to collect his wallet and his checkbook. He felt unhappy about leaving his new Corvette, but figured he could send someone for it in the morning. He wanted to be on his bike. He wanted to feel the wind on his face, the miles passing under him. He planned on riding all the way to the coast, where so many girls thought the imaginary Mack Slate composed his wonderful murder mysteries. This time he had a story to tell.

Marvin drove half the night before he caught the salty whiff of the Pacific Ocean. He ended up in a small seaside town called Forest—appropriately enough, its few buildings were surrounded by deep forest. There he stayed at a tiny motel called Fred's House. He slept to noon the next day, and when he

162

awoke he left and rented a cottage overlooking the crashing waves. Next he drove to a neighboring town called Tabott, which was a little larger than Forest, and where he was able to rent a computer and a printer. He had a devil of a time carrying them both back to his cottage on his motorcycle, but did manage.

The cottage was furnished. It even had a coffee-pot, always a good friend to a writer past his deadline. There was also a phone and he sat down and placed three calls. The first was to his sister Ann. He got her answering machine—she had her own phone. He left the message that he was all right, working on his book, and that she would see him Friday. Next he called his editor. He promised her she would have his manuscript in her hands Saturday; he would express-mail it to her home address and she'd be able to read it over the weekend. Finally he called big Ed, the guy who had sold him the Corvette. He described where the car was and promised Ed a couple of hundred if he'd pick it up and store it at the dealership until he returned for it on Friday. Ed was wise enough not to ask too many questions.

Then Marvin disconnected the phone.

There was a stereo in the living room and Marvin set up his computer at the kitchen table. He flipped the dial to the local rock station and turned the volume up high. He started to write.

Boy, did he write.

He sat at his computer, typing at warp speed, until his spine ached and his belly growled. Then he walked to a nearby store and bought a sandwich, a bag of potato chips, and a Coke. But he didn't loiter. He didn't talk to anybody. He didn't stop to stare in any store windows. He walked straight back to his cottage and sat down at his computer.

The plot of his book thickened. Clyde began to suspect that his best friend, Terry, had killed Ann. But Clyde didn't tell anybody, not even the reader, and a few pages later he turned up dead in the same lake where Ann's body had been found. Outside the cottage the sun set and then came back up, and Marvin went for another sandwich. The plot deepened. Sweet Mike—who had had sex with Ann in front of a blazing fire—began to suspect that Clyde would not have committed suicide out of grief. Not a year after his girlfriend had died. Mike went to see Jessica, Ann's best friend—who had had sex with Clyde on the hood of her green Alfa Romeo. Mike tells Jessica of his suspicions. Then Mike and Jessica fall in love—right in the middle of their conversation. Jessica is, after all, as beautiful as Ann was. She was getting better-looking every few paragraphs.

But by then Marvin was exhausted, and he lay down and slept for a few hours. When he awoke Mike and Jessica were kissing in a Jacuzzi and wondering why they had never noticed each other before. But they didn't have sex because they both suddenly remembered Ann and began to cry in each other's arms. They had sex the next night, however, when they were both feeling stronger. It was while lying beside Jessica that Mike came up with the idea that Ann had not died in Silver Lake, but had died hanging from a bridge that stretched over a river that ran into the lake. He didn't wake Jessica and tell her, however. He loved to look at her while she was sleeping.

Somewhere in the middle of Mike's analysis of Ann's death Marvin had to rest again. He was enjoying writing from Mike's point of view more than ever. The guy was having a lot of good times with Jessica and Mike was a lot like him. In fact, Mike probably *was* him—if the mirror theory of his series and his life was accurate. Yet he already knew that it was only partially true. Harry Paster's murder had inspired Ann McGaffer's murder. Sesa had planted the seed of Silver Lake. But a parallel was not the same as a copy. There were more people in the book than he knew in real life.

And still he didn't know how the book would end.

The days rolled into one long spin of the earth around the sun. He drank pots of coffee, ate sandwiches from the deli, and occasionally walked along the beach. The sound of the crashing waves revived him when he was most exhausted. He was in a tunnel of concentration he had been in before, but never had he been driving so fast. Yet he felt the *power*. He had been within inches of death and survived—what a rush—and as Mack Slate he controlled the destinies of everyone in Silver Lake.

Back at the computer. Back in Mike's mind. Mike visited Jessica unexpectedly and found her making passionate love to Terry in the backyard next to the doghouse. Poor Mike—he was devastated. He wanted revenge. He wanted to kill them both, but Terry first because there was still a possibility that Mike would make love to Jessica one more time—before he killed her, of course. Jessica—who was not only Ann's best friend, but her alter ego as well. Mike came up with a plan to destroy Terry, taking bits and pieces of how Ann had been destroyed. Yet Mike didn't understand that Terry was the ultimate villain. Mike only knew that he felt *good* about plotting Terry's murder, when only a couple of months before he couldn't have hurt a fly.

But that was the key—inside and outside the series. Where do you get your ideas from, Mr. Slate? He could finally answer that one, he thought. The stories were all a subconscious interpretation of reality. Can you dig that? Sweet Mike of Silver Lake fame could. He sold Terry a motorcycle and told him he could pick up the registration slip in a nearby town—on the other side of the bridge.

But Terry asked Jessica to come with him, and Jessica went because she believed her plot to catch the dastardly Mike had finally come to fruition. Yes, sad as it was to reveal the truth to millions of teenagers but Jessica had been plotting against Mike from the opening sentence of the last book, and the only reason she had slept with him was that it was required of her.

Late Thursday night Marvin brought his characters to their final confrontation on the bridge. By early Friday morning Mike was able to escape the deadly arena, with the other two at each other's throats.

Yet Sweet Mike was not happy.

He still had things on his mind.

So did Marvin.

Marvin sat back from his computer and wondered if Shelly was OK.

He had come within maybe five pages of the end of the book. He could go no further until he returned to Sesa. He checked the time. It was two in the morning. It would take him an hour to spell-check his work. The printer he had rented was a letter-quality dot matrix. It would take three hours to print out the entire manuscript, during which time he could sleep. If he woke at, say, six o'clock, it would be nine o'clock in New York and his agent and editor would be in their respective offices. Then, with a few calls, he could get a new ball rolling in his life.

Marvin finished cleaning up the book and started printing it. He had tentatively titled it *The Mystery of Silver Lake VI—Night of Grief*. He crashed on the sofa in the living room. When the noise of the printer stopped, it would wake him.

He slept well, for the three hours. He always did when one of his books was printing.

"Hello, Ben? This is Marvin. I've decided to accept that offer to fly down to Hollywood to meet with the director and the producer. Can you arrange things for me? Great, yeah, we'll finally get to meet. I'm sure neither of us will look the way the other thought. What was that? Oh, those letters. Yeah, I found out who was sending them. Just some young girl. You don't have to worry about her. I'll talk to you soon."

But Marvin was worrying more and more about

Shelly. It was as if getting all the recent events out of his system and onto paper had given him a more genuine perspective on things.

I did leave her in the hands of a murderer.

Marvin called his editor next.

"Hello, Pat? Rejoice. The book is done. Hear it printing in the background? That's it. No, I'm not just telling you that. You will see it tomorrow morning. You will know who killed Ann McGaffer. You can't wait? All right, I'll tell you right now. Just kidding! Hey, Pat, I thought of this great promotional idea. I want your publicity department to contact the media out here and have them come to a reading of excerpts from the final installment in the Silver Lake series. I want to do the reading at a local high school called Sesa High. It's in Oregon. That's where I live, yeah. You like the idea? I thought you would. I want to do the reading this afternoon. Yeah, today, at noon. Sure your people can arrange it. Why not? It'll just take a few phone calls. No, I'm not going to read the part that explains who killed Ann McGaffer! Do you think I'm crazy? What? I feel it's time I came out of the closet. It's getting stuffy in here. I agree—I deserve more personal recognition. The reading's got to be this afternoon. The principal at the high school must be contacted promptly. He's to notify the student body that I will do a signing after the reading so that all the kids can bring their books. I realize I might have to sign a thousand books. I don't care, it'll be fun. The principal and the media must be told that my real name is Marvin Summer. That must come from you, not from me. That is very important. That's my real name. Really. Monday will be too late. Why? Because, Pat, this story is not just any story."

A few minutes later Marvin set the phone down.

Pat said she would get on it right away.

It was time to go home.

BATTLE OF BILLIARDS

vers imported. That's ridiculous. Really. You
do well before this. Word. Besides, Jim, imports is
not just any sport.

A few minutes later, Marvin set the phone down.
He said she would get on a night later.

It was time to go inside.

CHAPTER 14

Marvin rode through Pella on his way back and collected his shiny red Corvette. He left his motorcycle at the dealership with Ed and asked the sales manager to have the bike delivered to his house later in the day. Naturally he tipped Ed handsomely for his efforts.

He got home at ten past eleven in the morning. Ann was waiting outside on the porch for him. She almost jumped out of her skin when he drove up—she was so excited. She launched herself into his arms as he stood up outside his car.

"I missed you!" she cried, burying her face in his shoulder and hugging him tighter than he deserved. He felt a stab of guilt. He should have called and spoken to her directly and put her mind more at ease.

170

"I missed you, too," he said.

"What's with the car?" she asked.

"It's mine. I bought it."

"Really? That's cool."

"How's Mom?" he asked.

Ann let go of him and bounced on tiptoes. "She's not drinking. She hasn't had a drink since you punched out Dad."

Marvin felt a rush of pure delight. "Really?"

"Yeah. Her brain's working again. I hardly know her."

"What made all this happen?"

Ann shrugged. "I don't know. I think she got scared that night. Oh, Dad's in jail. The police came right after you ran out of the house and arrested him for breaking our TV. They're going to keep him in jail for ninety days."

Ninety days. Three months. Marvin would be eighteen by then and in full control of his bank accounts. His father wouldn't be able to touch them while he was behind bars. So his money was safe. He didn't have to hide anymore.

Of course, he had already made the decision to come out of the closet before he had known of his father's imprisonment. The truth of the matter was that he had been ready to take on his father if the guy had tried to take his money. He was tired of cowering behind his pen name. He had almost been looking forward to the legal battle. But it was probably better this way, much better if it meant his mother had been shocked into going straight. Perhaps being in the slammer would sober up his father. Marvin didn't really dislike the guy. He just felt sorry for him.

"I finished my book," Marvin said casually.

Ann squealed. "All of it?"

"I'm down to the last few pages."

"Is it bitchin'?"

"The best."

She hugged him again. "You are the best. You're my big brother."

"I'm going to read from the book at school today. The TV and the newspapers are going to be there. I'm going to do a book signing and interviews."

Ann almost fainted dead away. "I can tell all my friends you're Mack Slate?"

He laughed. "Yeah. Tell everybody."

"Tell everybody what?" his mother asked, coming out the front door. If Ann hardly knew her anymore, Marvin hardly recognized her. It was as if she had gained ten pounds in the last week. Her dark hair had shine to it and the lines on her face were almost gone. But the biggest change was in her eyes. They were clear, they were alert. He walked over and gave her a hug.

"You look wonderful," he said.

She let go of him and smiled. "I feel wonderful."

"You're not going to start drinking again because I've come home?"

She laughed and socked him. He couldn't remember the last time he had heard her laugh. "You nut. You've had Ann and me worried to death. Where have you been for the last week?"

"I was in a small town called Forest. It's on the coast."

"What were you doing there?" His mom pointed at his Corvette. "And where did you get that car?"

Marvin spoke seriously. "I bought the car at a dealership in Pella. I got the money for it from books I've written. That's what I was doing in Forest—writing the final book in a series I've been developing for the last year."

His mother was bewildered. "What are you talking about? What books?"

Ann flashed a grin that went from ear to ear. "Have you ever heard of Mack Slate, Mom?" she asked.

Their mother paused. "Isn't he that novelist who writes those scary teenage stories?"

Ann pointed at Marvin. "He's your son."

Their mom still didn't get it, and it wasn't because of any lingering alcohol in her system. The news would have been too much for any mother to comprehend.

"I heard on the news that Mack Slate was going to be in town this afternoon," she muttered. "Is that what you're talking about?"

"He's always been in town," Marvin said, squeezing his mother once more. "But now he's back to stay. Don't worry, I'll explain everything later. Right now Ann and I have to go to my school."

"They've called a couple of times looking for you," his mom said.

"They're looking for me now," Marvin agreed.

Sesa High was abuzz with anticipation. Marvin and his sister got there a few minutes before lunch started and already half the student body was loitering in the halls. They had never had a celebrity visit before—certainly not one who had touched them so directly. Everywhere Marvin and Ann walked people were asking, "Did you hear? God, why is he coming to this dump?" They were so excited they didn't even stop to ask Marvin why he had his little sister with him, or why he had a manuscript tucked under his right arm. Although Marvin had not specified it during his conversation with his editor, he was happy to see the principal had not yet revealed Mack Slate's true identity. At least two TV stations were setting up equipment in the gym. The gossip was that Mack Slate was going to reveal ahead of time who had killed Ann McGaffer.

Marvin discreetly inquired as to the whereabouts of Shelly and Triad. He got nowhere. Apparently neither had been in class all week. At least no bodies had been found floating in the lake.

"Why is Shelly missing?" Ann asked, following him everywhere he went. She was so excited. Her green eyes were big.

"I don't know," Marvin said, and now there was no denying his disquiet. But why did he care? She had used him. She deserved whatever happened to her. Yet he prayed it had not been too final.

Lunch started and every student on campus headed straight for the gymnasium. Half of them had Mack Slate titles in hand; many must have dashed home between periods to get their books. Marvin and Ann followed the river of people, but neither took a seat in the stands once they were inside the old building, where for the last four years Sesa High had managed to lose ninety percent of its basketball games, another small detail he had managed to work into his plot. Marvin spotted their principal, Mr. Peters, who waved and came over. Mr. Peters had been on the verge of retirement for the last twenty years, but somehow managed to come up with a fresh birth certificate for the local board of education every time his contract came up for renewal. He loved working with kids.

"In all my fifty years teaching I have never been so stunned as I was this morning when I got that call from New York," Mr. Peters said, beaming. He offered his hand—both his bony hands—and gave Marvin a vigorous shake. "Congratulations. You know this place is going to fall apart when I tell them who you are."

"Have you told anybody?" Marvin asked.

"A couple of the TV people know," Mr. Peters said, glancing over at a remote crew that Marvin realized was a network. National coverage! Yet he shouldn't have been surprised. The debate over who had killed Ann McGaffer had been raging in major newspapers across the country for the last three months.

"I wonder if anybody will believe you when you say who I am," Marvin said.

"They will," Ann piped up. "I can vouch for you."

It took fifteen minutes for the crowd to settle down. Many had food with them, but few were eating. Gazes kept flicking to the entrance. Where is he? What does he look like? What famous starlet will he arrive with on his arm? Marvin saw Sandy, the redhead from Mr. Ramar's class who thought Mack Slate was still suffering from a love affair that hadn't worked out. Then there was blond Debra who believed Mack Slate had a whole cute family of blondes to keep him company. Mr. Ramar and Mrs. Jackson were sitting together in the front row. Occasionally all four of these people would look at him speaking with Mr. Peters, but none of them paid much attention to him. Mr. Peters leaned over and spoke in Marvin's ear.

"How do you want to be introduced?" the principal asked.

Marvin glanced down at Ann. "What do you think?" he asked.

"You should be introduced as my big brother," Ann said with a straight face.

Marvin chuckled and then was thoughtful for a moment. "Tell them you'd like to introduce Marvin Summer, who writes the Mack Slate books. That's all. You don't have to say anything else."

"That's true," Mr. Peters said, understanding. "They know who you are. Do you want to take questions? Or give a brief talk? Or read from your new book?"

"I'll talk for a couple of minutes," Marvin said. "I don't want to give a speech. I'll take a few questions. Then I'll read and sign books."

A hush settled over the audience as Mr. Peters stepped to the microphone. The lights from the TV cameras went on, flooding the basketball court in eerie brilliance. Marvin continued to search the stands for Shelly or Triad. He could have been straining to think up the ending of his series. He would just have to wait, and let it come—one or the other, or neither. Sometimes the best ending was to have nothing at all happen. Sometimes it was the saddest.

Mr. Peters cleared his throat. "Ladies and gentlemen. It is my great pleasure to introduce a young man you have known for years. Let's have a big hand for Marvin Summer, author of the Mack Slate thrillers."

The place did not erupt at the announcement. The opposite occurred—the silence deepened. Marvin could have heard a pin drop as he walked to the microphone. The glare from the lights half blinded him but he noted that Sandy from Mr. Ramar's class had fainted dead away. Mrs. Jackson was not doing much better. She had her head down between her knees and Mr. Ramar was anxiously checking on her. Marvin remembered that Mrs. Jackson had been working on a novel for the last ten years but had been unable to get it published. The rest of the people were frozen in place. Marvin didn't know where to begin so he just started talking.

"Hi," he said. "I feel self-conscious at the moment. I like to think that I know most of you here, but that none of you have really known me. Since my books were published, I've walked around this campus feeling smug. I'd see some of you with my titles and I'd think, they don't know I created that. They don't know how great I am. Really, I was conceited. But I think I've gotten over that. The last few days some things have happened and I've begun to realize everybody's got a story, and that I was mistaken to think that I was the only one. That's all I wanted to say, besides thank you for reading my books. I write because I love to tell stories, and it makes me happy to see people enjoying my stories." Marvin paused. "Are there any questions?"

About a hundred people raised their hands. Marvin pointed to a girl in the front row. She stood. She had a copy of the first Silver Lake book in her hands. He knew what she was going to ask before she opened her mouth.

"Where do you get your ideas, Mr. Slate?" she asked.

Marvin laughed. "From you. From all of you."

There were more questions, tons of them. They wanted to know how he had managed to keep his identity secret. How much money he made. How long it took him to write a book. Whether any of the people in his books were based on people he knew—on *them*. Marvin laughed again at the last question and sat down and began to read the beginning of the last installment of *The Mystery of Silver Lake*.

" 'Mike Madison sat in class watching the beautiful Jessica Moss putting lipstick on her wide sensual mouth. Jessica was two seats up on his right, and she was reading a Hollywood sex novel. She looked as if she was really into the book. Every other page her cheeks would turn red and her breathing would accelerate. Mike suspected she was reading *nasty* parts, and he wondered if Jessica was feeling particularly hard up. Mike sure was. He had not been with a girl since Ann McGaffer. That had been a year ago, only two days before Ann had died. . . .'"

Later Marvin spoke to the people from the media and signed several hundred books. Sandy, the redhead, slipped him her number after he had inscribed each book in her Mack Slate collection. She appeared to have recovered nicely from her collapse. Debra, the blonde, also gave him her number. In fact, she invited him over for dinner that night. She wanted him to meet her parents. Marvin supposed she was still dreaming of Mr. Slate's little blond babies.

Marvin kept the numbers. What the hell, he thought.

Mrs. Jackson was one of the last people to approach him. By then it was close to four o'clock; he had been signing all afternoon. In her hand she carried the first novel he had published—*The Wishing Web*. He didn't want to rub it in so he just opened the book to sign the title page. He was surprised to see it already had an inscription.

For Marvelous Marvin!
  I just read this book while waiting.
  It's great.
  An A+ Three A+++!!!

Congratulations!
Your humble English teacher.

Mary.

"Wait till you read my Seymour the Frog series," Marvin remarked.

Mrs. Jackson was a good sport. "I can hardly wait," she said.

EPILOGUE

But Shelly Quade never appeared, not even at the end of the line as Marvin had dreamed she would. He finished the day by accepting a few more girls' phone numbers and then slipped out with his sister. Ann kept shaking her head. It had been the happiest day of her life. She could hardly wait to read his new book.

"I still have a few pages to do," he warned.

"When are you going to do them?" she asked.

"Soon. Tonight."

He was home, sitting in front of his computer screen after a nice family dinner with his mom and sister, when he felt a sudden urge to go for a walk. He left the house—this time he said goodbye to everybody—and got on his bike and drove to Sesa Lake. It was dark and cold but the air was still oddly serene. There was no one around. He walked along the shore he had walked the previous Friday evening before his date with Shelly, even so far as the west end, where the hills met the water and the cliff stood that had supposedly been the instrument of Harry Paster's death. Somehow he was going to have to tell Harry's grief-stricken mother that her son had not committed suicide, without telling her how he knew. Perhaps he could give her a copy of his series to read. So many secrets between those carefully worded lines.

He was sitting with his feet dangling over the cliff, the water flat and black a hundred feet below, when he heard a sound off to his left. He looked up to find a white figure approaching. A girl, a pretty girl. The world was full of them, but there weren't too many like this one.

"Hi," she said when she was closer.

"Hello, Shelly," he said. "How are you?"

She came and sat beside him. "Fine. How are you?"

"Excellent." He paused. "Are you armed?"

"Marvin." She allowed a soft laugh. She was three feet away and it was so dark she was nothing but a silhouette. "I have your knife."

"Can I have it?"

"Maybe." She scooted a little closer. He could have reached out and put his arm around her. If he had wanted to. "I've missed you this last week," she said.

"Everybody's missed you. Where have you been?"

"Here and there. Waiting for you to return."

"You didn't have to wait," he said.

"You're not going to talk?"

He shrugged. "Who am I going to talk to?"

Shelly sighed but didn't say anything. They stared at the water for a while. Finally she spoke. "Do you want to know what happened?"

"Sure. I'm a sucker for a mystery. Start at the beginning."

She lowered her head. She was not dressed warmly: a thin white sweater. But the cold had never seemed to bother her. He was surprised when she suddenly shivered.

"I thought you killed him," she began. "I guess you know that already. But I didn't think it at first, at least not consciously. I just didn't want to be around you. I missed Harry so much, and there was something about you that reminded me of him. Even then, though, I knew you were Mack Slate. I'd known since the third time we went out. I'd read *The Wishing Web* when we started dating, and the way you talked, and the way the book was written —they were the same. Do you know what I mean?"

He nodded. "They had the same voice."

"Yes. But I didn't know for sure. But then all those wonderful stories you used to tell me—right off the top of your head—that made me wonder, too. So much that I snuck into your house one day when nobody was home and turned on your computer. Then I knew." She paused. "Does that make you mad?"

"You tried to have me killed, Shelly. The fact that you also snooped around my room doesn't exactly shock me."

She chewed on that a moment. "I see your point. But you're wrong to think I wanted you killed. That would have been easy. But I was telling you my story. Where was I? The summer after Harry died—last summer—your series was out, and I read it. Right away I was struck by how you had worked Harry's death into the plot, exchanging Ann McGaffer for Harry. But then I read the second book, and the people, the circumstances, the events—I began to see that you *were* writing about what had happened to Harry."

"You saw more than I did," Marvin quipped.

"I find that hard to believe."

Marvin shrugged again. "I'm not going to try to convince you."

She stared at him a moment. "The series made me realize that the only way you could have known so much about how Harry died was to have killed him. So last summer I began to suspect you. But I didn't do anything. I wasn't sure. But the third book came out, and then the fourth and fifth, and each added more detail, and gave me more confidence that you were the culprit. It was then I decided I needed to test you."

"But that's crazy. Why would I have killed Harry?"

"For the same reason Mike Madison killed Ann McGaffer."

"But Mike didn't kill Ann," Marvin said impatiently. "Terry did."

"I didn't know that. I hadn't read the last book."

"Why didn't you wait till it came out? Then you

could have bought it at any bookstore and known for sure. What was the matter? Were you too cheap to spring for the four bucks?"

Shelly was indignant. "I am not cheap. You didn't know it was Triad—I mean, Terry who killed Ann until last week. You've said that much yourself. You couldn't have written about it unless everything that happened on the bridge between us happened."

"Oh, so now I suppose I owe you some of my royalties."

"That wouldn't be a bad idea," she snapped back.

"Shelly."

"I'm saying that you have been writing about this whole business from the beginning and that my suspicion of you was natural." Shelly stopped to take a breath. She looked back down at the water and continued in a lower voice. "I thought you killed Harry because you were jealous of him. Because you were in love with me and wanted me for yourself."

"You have a high opinion of yourself, don't you?"

She whirled his way. "I think I was right. At least half right."

"A little knowledge is a dangerous thing."

"You're good with one-liners, aren't you?"

He shrugged. "Whole paragraphs. Go on. You decided you had to test me. What next?"

"I came at you two ways. I sent you the fan letter that said *I know you.* I knew you would notice that

185

it had been mailed locally. Because I was going on the assumption you had killed Harry, I thought it would make you anxious and paranoid."

"It did that and I hadn't even killed anybody."

"You see, it worked. I wanted you to feel paranoid about the letters, but I wanted you to trust them as well. So that I could use them to direct you to act when I wanted you to act. But my second note was designed to make you suspicious of me. I knew you would come to my house Saturday night once you picked up the *third* note I stuffed in your box that evening."

"How did you know that I had picked up the note? I only went to the post office by chance."

"I figured there was a good chance you would. I staked out the place with Triad. Once you had it in your hand we hurried back to my house and got in the Jacuzzi."

"The sacrifices you made in the line of duty."

"It was all staged. None of it meant a thing to me."

"You were groaning naked in his arms," he said.

"I wasn't naked. I had my bathing suit on. It was hidden by the bubbles. The only reason I was groaning was because I knew you were watching. I could see you in the mirror in the den. I was happy, at the time, that you stood there so long. That was when I really got to pull your strings."

"Wait a second. How did Triad get involved in all this?"

"He was Harry's best friend," Shelly said. "I needed help setting you up. It was normal that I should have approached him for assistance." She stopped and rubbed her head—all of a sudden it seemed to be hurting her. "I see now why he was so anxious to help me."

"That's an understatement."

"Would you just listen to me and try to understand?" she asked, a note of desperation entering her voice. It was rare that Shelly ever sounded emotional. Not for the first time he wondered what had happened while he was working on his book. He was relieved to see she was alive, but he still hated her for the way she had used him.

"I'm listening," he said in a flat voice.

She spoke as if she was trying to convince herself. "This whole test of mine was necessary to clear Harry's name and give me peace of mind. I had ample evidence that you had killed Harry in a jealous rage. Then when I made you jealous again, you acted exactly as I thought you would. You tried to kill Triad. You even used the way I thought you used to kill Harry."

"You knew that I would be waiting there to trip the bike?"

"I suspected you'd be," Shelly said.

"But how did you know that way had been used before?"

She looked at him as if he were slow. "I read about it in your books."

"That's right. I forgot." In going back through the earlier books in the series he had discovered that he had already written in an old piece of rope hanging from the bridge. He'd had little patchwork to do to accommodate his surprising new ending. Not that he had finished writing the end. He needed a few more facts. He was talking to just the person who could give them to him. "I'm with you so far," he said. "Whether I want to be or not. But you've skipped over a crucial part of the story."

"What really happened last year?"

"Yeah. Do you know?"

"Yes."

"Tell me."

"All right." She reached in her back pocket and pulled out a shiny silver object. Marvin recognized his knife. He wondered if there was a special significance in her timing. He stirred uncomfortably, although she didn't appear in a threatening mood. Shelly continued. "Harry was jealous of you. He knew I was going out with you—I had told him. But I hadn't told him how I felt about you. Maybe he guessed; I don't know. Anyway, he got drunk with Triad that Friday night we were out celebrating your birthday. You know how people get when they're drunk. Their miseries either vanish or magnify a hundredfold. The latter must have happened to Harry. He told Triad how pissed he was at you, how he wanted to get back at you. Triad was sympathetic. He told Harry that he'd overheard that you were going to see a late movie in Pella that night, and that you would be crossing the bridge around midnight if they wanted to spring a little surprise on you."

"Did Triad tell Harry that you were with me?" Marvin asked.

"No."

Marvin nodded. "I didn't know you'd be with
̣d last week."

Shelly was taken aback. "Didn't you see me on the back of the bike when we were on our way to Pella?"

"No, I was too far from the road. Go on."

"Triad and Harry got a piece of rope and a can of oil and headed out to the bridge," Shelly said. "Harry was far more drunk than Triad. In fact, Triad was in complete control. He knew exactly what he was doing. This was the opportunity he had been waiting for. He thought he could kill two birds with one stone. You see Harry had made a fatal mistake when he had confided in Triad about how jealous he was of you."

"Because Triad was also in love with you," Marvin interrupted.

Shelly was impressed. "How did you know?"

"It's in the book I just wrote."

"Seriously? How did you know to write that?"

"I could see it in Triad's eyes on the bridge."

"Even as he was smashing my head into the railing?"

"Especially then," Marvin said with a note of bitterness. "You forget, I know from experience what jealousy can drive a man to do."

She ignored his tone. "Harry set the rope up. Or maybe Triad set it up, I don't know. But it was Harry who went over the side of the railing with the rope around his waist. He sat there waiting in the cold for you to come by, ready to trip you off your bike. But then you came by with me on the back and he realized his mistake. At the last second he let the rope drop." She paused. "Harry wasn't a killer."

"I believe you," he said sarcastically.

She was angry. "You're the last person in the world who can take that tone with me."

He didn't snap back. "I also lowered the rope when I saw you were on the back," he said. "I think I would have lowered it if you hadn't been on the back."

"Really?"

"Didn't you hear me shout out?"

"No," she said. "Triad wanted to wear the helmet. The wind was strong in my ears and my eyes. Triad was going to brake all along. He'd had a bike a couple years ago—he knew how to stop them in nothing flat."

"I could see that." Marvin realized there was a big hole in her story. "When Triad was getting Harry drunk and talking him into wasting me, did he know you would be returning from Pella with me?"

Shelly didn't hesitate. "Yes."

"But then he was risking you? I don't understand."

Her voice was cold. "Don't you? You say you didn't know I was on the back of the bike last week. All right, I believe you. But why didn't you know? Were you afraid to look when we were on the way to Pella in case I was?"

She had turned the tables on him quickly. "No. Like I said, I was too far from the road, and then I dropped my binoculars in the river and . . ." Marvin heard his voice trail off. He supposed he might have been trying to avoid the issue, until it was too late. But it was hard to imagine he could have been so cold-blooded. He added, "I don't think I really wanted to hurt you."

"Last year Triad didn't care if I died along with you," Shelly said. "If he couldn't have me, no one was going to have me. I'm sure he had it all figured out. He would have made sure Harry took the rap for our deaths. Last Sunday Triad didn't care that it wasn't part of the plan to have you die."

It was his turn to get back at her. "Are you sure that wasn't part of *your* plan? I came awfully close to going in that water."

Shelly spoke firmly. "I figured I could go to the police and tell them you had tried to kill Triad and me, and that you had probably killed Harry. I would have had Triad as a witness. That was my goal from the beginning—to make you pay for what you had done. Look, we both screwed each other. That's the way it is. You keep acting like you're my moral superior, but there's no difference between us."

"There is a big difference," Marvin said. "You drove me to do what I did. You started it."

"Because I thought you had started it," Shelly snapped.

"But I didn't start it. You made the wrong assumption. You *were* wrong."

"And you were right to string a rope across a bridge in front of an oncoming motorcycle?"

Marvin was getting tired of the argument. It kept going in circles. "Finish your story," he said.

"Harry dropped the rope and we went by. Triad went running to him and shoved Harry off the edge of the bridge. Triad hung him, by his armpits. He let him hang there all weekend. Triad even went and played in the football game while Harry was trapped under the bridge." Shelly sniffed. "Harry must have been dead, though, when the rope finally snapped and he fell in the river. I hope he was dead."

Marvin found it difficult to speak for a moment, the image was so gruesome. But he had to know. "Go on," he said.

"You know the rest. You saw on the bridge how Triad showed his true colors. I was as surprised as you. More so." She touched her head again. "What a fool I was. The bastard was right in front of me all along and I couldn't see it. Especially after I knew—Oh, never mind."

"Especially after you knew what?"

She twisted her face into an odd expression. "Especially after I knew that the Terry in your books had been out drinking with the Clyde in your books not long before Clyde turned up dead."

Marvin snorted. "Ain't that a coincidence."

A silence settled between them. Marvin could feel the damp from the ground seeping into his lower body. It was getting late. It didn't look like his editor would be getting the book tomorrow morning as he had promised. Oh, well, she should be thankful Shelly hadn't sneaked up on him in the dark and slit his throat. Then he wouldn't have been able to write any more best-sellers.

The dampness was haunting. The ground they were sitting on had been disturbed recently—dug up.

"What are you thinking?" Shelly asked finally.

He picked up a stone and tossed it into the water far below. He heard the initial splash but not the spreading ripples. Those he had to imagine—spreading over the entire lake, touching every part of the shore. His stories were like that. They burst without control from his imagination and reappeared in a million printed replicas in bookstores. Maybe they touched too many minds, in the wrong places. He had never thought about that before. He glanced at the knife resting in Shelly's lap.

His knife.

But with whose blood on it?

"I used to have a nightmare about this lake when I was a kid," he said. "I'd be walking along the shore at night and I'd hear a monster rising from the depths. I'd try to run away, but no matter which way I ran I'd continue to circle the water. The monster would surface, and come up at my back, ready to pounce. But each time I had this dream there would be this flash of red light, and I would wake up beside the lake in the daytime. Only I would still be dreaming because the lake would be dried-up and human bones would be strewn all over the cracked lake bed." He paused. "What do you think a dream like that means?"

Shelly spoke carefully. "That you imagine there are secrets here that are hidden."

"A psychiatrist would agree with that analysis." Marvin nodded to himself. "Why did you come here tonight?"

"I was there this afternoon when you held your assembly."

"You didn't answer my question," he said.

"I wanted to talk to you. I thought you might be here."

"Why did you think I would be here?" he asked.

She was shrewd. No wonder she had been able to penetrate his disguise and manipulate him so easily. She understood the way his mind worked. But then, he was beginning to understand how her mind worked. His Ann McGaffer, and her alter ego, his Jessica Moss. She was both of them, really, rolled into one neat package.

"Tell me why you came here," she said.

"Because this is where it all began," he said. "And I still have to write the end of my book."

"And you thought this might be where it all ends?" she asked.

"Yeah."

Shelly picked up the knife. She studied it in the dark. Not a ghostly glimmer of light shone on the silver blade. Yet he knew it must be cold to the touch.

"Do you want it?" she asked.

"Are you offering it to me?"

"Maybe."

"You said that a few minutes ago." He was much stronger than she, even unarmed. He shouldn't be in any danger. Yet he continued to follow the hand that held the knife. She had it in her right, which she was keeping near the ground, in the grass, partially behind him. He wouldn't be very strong if she stabbed him and he were losing a pint of blood a minute. He added, "I don't know where it's been."

"Are you afraid to get your fingerprints on it?"

She leaned closer and her eyes glistened with the sheen of moisture. Her mood had changed once more. She could turn it on and off. She was back in control. The powerful mysterious Shelly he so loved writing about. "Are you afraid, Marvin?"

"Was Triad afraid?"

"Yes," she said.

"How did you get the knife away from him?"

Shelly brushed his hair from his forehead with her free hand. He could feel her breath on the side of his cheek. "I kissed him," she said.

"I see."

"Do you want me to kiss you?"

He considered a moment. "Maybe."

She brushed the side of his cheek with her lips. "What would Mack Slate do?" she asked.

He considered longer. It was her game. It had been from the beginning, even though he had written the rules.

"Yes," he whispered.

She kissed him. She tasted as she always had— like love. Crazy as it seemed he still loved her. She was as corrupt as he. She kissed him hard. Then she pulled back and smiled.

"You have balls," she said.

"Two of them. You should kiss me again."

She did. And when she was done, she said, "Triad didn't."

"No?"

"No," she said.

"Did you kill him?" he asked.

"I can't tell you that."

"Why not? I know everything else."

"If I tell you that I would have to kill you," she said.

"But I don't know how to end my book."

She laughed softly. And Shelly's soft laughs always felt to him like a hot knife sliding into butter. They always made him melt.

"You know he told me everything I just told you," she said. "And I can tell you he didn't want to tell me."

"But he was afraid not to?" he asked.

"Yes." She pulled away from him and lifted a handful of the loose soil they were sitting on. With her left hand. She continued to keep the knife in her right hand. She let the soil pour through her open fingers. "He had a right to be afraid," she said.

"And that's one body that will never be found," he whispered.

"I didn't say that," she said quickly.

He didn't feel like arguing with her. Ever again, for that matter. "I didn't hear you say it."

She gestured to the lake. "Why did you choose to come to this spot?"

He spoke carefully. "I wanted a soft spot to sit."

She brushed the dirt off her hand. She batted her eyelashes—no, her gaze strayed downward. Involuntarily. A lot of what they had done lately had been involuntary. He wondered himself why he had chosen the exact spot where she had buried Triad to stop and rest.

"You know enough to finish it," she said.

"I suppose. Will you let me?"

His question caught her by complete surprise.

"Sure. If you put in a sentence at the end about how the heroine did what she did in self-defense."

Marvin nodded. "I understand."

She laughed. "I'm glad." She took the knife and cast it far out into the water. He heard the splash. He imagined he saw the ripples as they rebounded on the farthest shore. He would have to watch them closer—in the future. She leaned close. "I want another kiss," she said.

He hesitated. "What's it going to cost me?"

She stroked his leg with her now free right hand. "A percentage of your royalties."

"How much?"

"A small percentage."

He put his arm around her shoulder. "I'd be crazy to be partners with you."

"That's why you're such a genius." She kissed him. "That's why I love you so much." She kissed him again. "Because you are totally nuts."

"That makes two of us."

"Ain't that the truth," Shelly agreed.

They ended up driving back to his house on his motorcycle. Once there they climbed in his Corvette and headed to the Portland Airport, four hours away. Because they were so late, they had to drop the manuscript off at the airport so that the package could make the final flight to New York. Shelly drove while he wrote the end of his book in longhand with the help of the car's overhead light. He figured his editor wouldn't mind a few pages handwritten. Especially when the last scene was so delightfully wicked. He didn't hold anything back.

Jessica slit Terry's throat wide open, and later in the same week had sex with Sweet Mike, this time in the backseat of a hot red sports car. Sitting beside him, Shelly said she didn't mind what he wrote.

"No one will believe it anyway," she said.

Marvin grinned. He was on the last page. Mike was having a good time. "We'll have to see if it *all* comes true," he said.

Look for Christopher Pike's

Monster

Coming in November 1992

About the Author

CHRISTOPHER PIKE was born in Brooklyn, New York, but grew up in Los Angeles, where he lives to this day. Prior to becoming a writer, he worked in a factory, painted houses, and programmed computers. His hobbies include astronomy, meditating, running, playing with his nieces and nephews, and making sure his books are prominently displayed in local bookstores. He is the author of *Last Act, Spellbound, Gimme a Kiss, Remember Me, Scavenger Hunt, Final Friends* 1, 2, and 3, *Fall into Darkness, See You Later, Witch, Die Softly, Bury Me Deep, Whisper of Death, Chain Letter 2: The Ancient Evil,* and *Master of Murder,* all available from Archway Paperbacks. *Slumber Party, Weekend, Chain Letter, The Tachyon Web,* and *Sati*—an adult novel about a very unusual lady—are also by Mr. Pike.